COTSWOLD
MURDERS

Also by Michael Spicer

Final Act
Prime Minister Spy
Cotswold Manners

Michael · Spicer

COTSWOLD
MURDERS

A THOMAS · DUNNE BOOK

St. Martin's Press New York

Design by Judith Stagnitto

Library of Congress Cataloging-in-Publication Data

Spicer, Michael.
    Cotswold murders / Michael Spicer.
        p.   cm.
    "A Thomas Dunne book."
    ISBN 0-312-04285-X
    I. Title.
PR6069.P498C64   1990
823'.914—dc20   90-8000
                                                             CIP

First Edition

10 9 8 7 6 5 4 3 2 1

To the memory of my sister Angela-Jane, who died in a car crash in South Africa in 1973.

Needless to say, all the characters in this book are totally fictitious and not meant to bear resemblance to any living person. Although the events take place in a very contemporary context, they, too, are all figments of my imagination.

COTSWOLD

MURDERS

1

Why is it, I wonder, that one's dreams often bear such a close resemblance to reality? I suppose one might add, which is which? Is the dream perhaps the real thing and the so-called reality the dream? Anything is surely possible within the infinity of space and time.

However, I have started on a note far too deep and profound for me to be able to keep up, quite out of character. The fact is that I never normally try to analyze anything that is not testable. As far as I am concerned, theories have to be *provable* one way or the other; when they are not, I work at once on gut feeling. It's partly the way I've been trained. There are occasions in my job when you simply don't have the time to sit around and ponder the unthinkable for too long. The habit can even become dangerous. Physically, I am rather petite and the quickness with which I react has usually been my best means of defense. If I had stopped too often to wonder why things were the way they were, I would no doubt be dead by now.

I have been prompted into this line of thought by the

fact that my story really begins at the point when I awoke from a dream. It was about a girl—no, more a young woman—who was being interviewed under hypnosis (something which we only do in my department if the subject freely agrees to it). During the course of the questioning, it became clear that the woman was a psychopath who carried a list of potential murder victims in her mind. I woke up just as she was confessing that my name was included on this list. The dream bore a striking resemblance in several respects to one of my cases, not the one I am recounting now but one that when I have the time I must also write up.

As I awakened, the girl on the opposite side of the railway compartment was staring directly at me. Her gaze had a sort of madness to it, like that of the woman in my dream. I adjusted my skirt, suddenly conscious that it was riding up my thighs, and then noted that the two of us were alone.

We were sitting in what was at that time something of a rarity on the Cotswold line, a railway carriage with compartments. Usually, British Rail provided us with aging High Speed 125 trains, retired from grander trunk routes and with open carriages laid out like the interior of an aeroplane except that the seats faced each other across plastic-topped tables.

On Sunday evenings, however, the railway authorities seemed to lose any incipient ambition to impress their customers with even the most modest of modern amenities. In place of the HS 125s, we were given rolling stock with heavy-cushioned sagging seats and dirty windows to match. Above each place, there was a chipped light that threw off the illumination of a gas lamp. The compartments had doors that slid backward and forward with the motion of the train. These opened onto narrow corridors;

invariably, they seemed filled with fat ladies and with men in uniform waving to sad little faces fading away on distant station platforms.

The particular day I am remembering was such a Sunday. As usual when I had stayed over the weekend at my cottage in Chipping Campden, I had been driven to Moreton-in-Marsh station by my septuagenarian bodyguard, the Honorable Patricia Huntington; and as usual, we had arrived in the small station yard at around ninety miles per hour (although I never actually look at the speedometer when Pat is driving). We got there just in time to catch the 19:34, which Pat called "the last decent train to London." It was an apt description: after this one, you had to change at Oxford and reached Paddington just after midnight.

Now fully awake, I began to focus on the rather surprising looks of my traveling companion opposite. Somehow these didn't quite fit with the fading pretensions of the first-class compartment in which we were sitting.

She had long brown hair that hung straight down to her shoulders. I put her age at between twenty-five and thirty; the darkness of her skin made it hard to tell with certainty. She might have been even older. Her face was not so much tanned as olive-colored. Every so often, she sniffed hard and rather irritatingly through a small, snubbed nose. Now that she saw that I was awake (I couldn't, incidentally, have been sleeping for more than ten minutes), her large round eyes switched away from me and she was staring out of the window onto the greens and golds of the Cotswold hills. These rolled past slowly in the clear summer-evening light as the train wound it's way carefully along the single track that links Kingham and Charlbury, before joining the main line at Oxford.

Her gaze was blank and vacant. I wondered whether she was engaged in deep meditation or whether perhaps she was just attracted by the sight of the sheep grazing in the patches of blue shadow thrown by the lush summer foliage.

As I looked more closely at her, I decided it was unlikely to be the sheep that were winning her attention. Her face was totally impassive; her eyes, in particular, when you looked at them carefully, were lifeless. The beauty of the landscape seemed to have failed entirely to reflect itself on her retina.

After a while, she began nervously to twist three copper bands that she wore on her right wrist under the sleeve of a thick black sweater. I thought I saw her shiver and remember thinking how odd this was, given the warmth of the carriage and the nature of the clothes she was wearing. It's true her legs were bare except for a pair of sandals, and a tight denim skirt stretched above her knees. However, I had on only a loose cotton dress with very little else underneath and I still felt uncomfortably warm. It was certainly an unusually hot evening for early June in England.

Her whole bearing was awkward. She sat uneasily, upright, with her legs held tightly together, a small silver cross on a chain around her neck. The thought ran through my mind that she couldn't have paid for her own ticket. The first-class fare was twice that of the second. Even I, with a generous allowance left to me by my late husband, with the additional salary I earned from the government, with houses in London and the Cotswolds and an apartment in New York, thought twice sometimes about the sense of spending the extra sixteen pounds return. The cushioning of the seats in second class was a little harder but that was about all; certainly there was just as much chance these days of having to stand in first class. The girl in front of me had no luggage and wasn't even carrying a handbag. She just didn't seem to be the type to travel first class out of her own resources.

I closed my eyes again, this time with no intention of falling asleep. After a few minutes, I opened them suddenly and without warning. As I had rather anticipated, she was staring straight at me again. Only this time, her eyes were brimming over with tears, one of which trailed down her right cheek. I felt rather embarrassed. I was being dragged into direct contact with her; at least that was how I began to see it at the time. What had so far been a mild interest on my part was becoming an involvement, so much so that I felt impelled to say something to her.

"You don't look very happy. Is there anything I can do to help?" I asked. She shook her head unsmilingly.

"I'm okay, thanks."

I thought I detected an Irish lilt in her voice. She had spoken too softly and had said too few words for me to be sure about this. At any rate, after this short exchange, we sat in silence. With some relief, I decided I had done my bit. I had at least made an effort to show some sympathy toward the poor girl.

I was not, however, to be let off so lightly. Ten minutes later, just as we were approaching Oxford with its distant college spires sparkling in the evening sunlight, she suddenly blurted out, "I need to talk to someone, anyone, so long as they don't know me and I don't know them."

"Will I do?" I offered, rather hoping she would say no.

She was distracted for a moment as the train began to draw alongside the platform. Then she turned back to me and said, "I won't talk if anyone else gets in here." She spoke very quietly and I still found her hard to hear. There was certainly a note of hysteria in her voice. There was, however, no doubt that my first impression had been right: She was Irish.

I looked out onto the platform. Unusually, there were very few people waiting—mainly young people in jeans with open-necked shirts and buttons undone down to their middles, wearing trilbies on the backs of their heads and woolen college scarves around their necks even on a hot night: students going up for late-night parties in London. As we came to a halt, they drifted off toward the back of the train and away from where we were sitting. After a few minutes, there was a sharp jolt and the train began to pull out and gather speed. It was now apparent that no one was going to join our compartment.

My fellow passenger seemed to have composed herself during the short stop. Her eyes were completely dry now. Suddenly, she leaned across to me and said in a voice that was perfectly calm and deeper than it had been before, "I've just killed someone."

I have been very highly trained to respond rationally to most conceivable situations, but this one to the best of my knowledge had not featured in any of the training manuals I had been given.

"What happened?" I asked. "Was it a driving accident?"

"I don't think you understand," she said. "I murdered someone."

"I see." I tried to remember exactly what they had taught us about gratuitous confessions.

"Have you told the police?" I asked.

She shook her head. The girl was probably slightly off her rocker; perhaps she had had a tiff with her boyfriend and was (with some success, I have to admit) trying to shock me to get my attention.

"But you're going to when we get to London?"

"To do what?"

"Tell the police."

"I doubt it. What good would that do?"

"What good has it done telling me?"

She shrugged. "I told you, you don't know me."

I thought for a moment and decided that I now had some responsibility in the matter, not just because I was a member of the security services but more as a simple citizen, at least to prove to my own satisfaction that she was talking gibberish.

"Where did you commit this murder?" I asked.

"In the Cotswolds." Now she seemed to be teasing me, or testing me out, perhaps to see at what point my resistance would break and I would properly engage myself in her problem.

"That's a big area. Doesn't give me much to go on, does it?"

She narrowed her eyes. Her glance for the first time appeared a little threatening.

"I didn't say I was trying to help you," she replied.

"No, I suppose not."

We fell into an uneasy silence, which for a moment was shattered by the howl of an express going in the opposite direction.

After a few minutes, she asked, "You don't believe me, do you?"

I paused before answering her. "I'm not sure yet."

"Hard to satisfy, aren't you? All right, I'll fill in a few details for you, just to pass the time until we get to London." It was a grudging concession and I wondered why she had made it. I looked at my watch: forty minutes to go if we were on time.

"Why not?" I said lightly. "We've got some time to kill before we reach Paddington and I haven't got anything else to do." I usually made a practice of using the one-and-a-half-hour journey to finish off routine reports for the chief. As it happened, on this occasion I had decided that the subject matter was too sensitive to risk doing on the train. I planned to work at it as soon as I reached my house in London.

"I'm Irish," she announced.

"That much I had worked out for myself."

She seemed not to notice my growing irritation with her, or possibly she chose just to ignore it.

"So I fell for this Paddy who happens to be a member of the Republican Army and is currently doing fifteen years in Top Marsden prison."

"You knew him before he was in prison?"

"Only as a friend of my elder brother. I fell for him after he was convicted."

"I know Top Marsden," I said.

She looked at me with a new interest.

"You don't look like the type to know about prisons," she said.

I was familiar with this one, partly because it was situated about ten miles from my cottage in Chipping Campden and partly because over a period of years I had conducted several difficult interrogations of prisoners there. I knew in particular that it was a maximum-security, high-technology prison, housing around 350 dangerous men, a number of whom were certainly members of the IRA.

"Is that where you've been today?" I asked. "Visiting your friend?"

She nodded. So far, she was making some sense; for instance, she had by inference explained her lack of luggage. She wouldn't have needed any for a day trip to Evesham, the nearest station to the prison. It didn't, of course, throw any light on why she was traveling first class. I knew that only second-class travel warrants were issued to prison visitors; we hadn't quite reached the point where Social Services considered that impoverished friends and relatives of prison inmates should travel first class at the taxpayer's expense.

"What's your friend's name?" I asked, and immediately

regretted the bluntness of the question. I reminded myself that she was no more to me than a fellow passenger and seemingly rather a pathetic one at that. It was absolutely not my business to subject her to any kind of interrogation. This sort of crime, if there had been one, was not even for my side of the house. My regret at having been so direct was well founded. She looked straight at me, her dark eyebrows furrowed in a look of hard suspicion.

"What's that to do with you?" she demanded.

"I'm sorry, it was rude of me. I shouldn't have interrupted you. I'm afraid I became rather carried away."

"Anyway," she added sulkily, "he's not much to do with me anymore. Told me today he wasn't interested in carrying on our relationship." The tears welled up in her eyes again.

Then, just as suddenly, her mood seemed to change again. The half-mocking tone returned to her voice. She said, "I doubt if someone as pretty as you has ever been jilted. Am I right? It wouldn't surprise me at all if it was all the other way round in your case. I bet it's always you who tells them to push off. I suppose it's all right by me as long as someone's fighting for our sex."

I had to admit to myself that she was not far off the mark about me, though for rather different reasons from the ones she gave. It was true that with the exception of the breakup of my marriage, when it had undoubtedly been my husband who had taken the offensive, it was more often than not I who had made the first move in ending a relationship with a man. It had nothing to do with my proving the superiority of my sex: Frankly, I just don't think in those terms. I may be physically tough, certainly capable of putting most men on the floor in thirty seconds, but that doesn't mean that I like to dominate them. On the contrary, when I am in the mood, I like nothing more than to be enveloped by a strong man. I like him to open doors for me and to wrap me in his arms and to lift me off my feet—not a superhuman task for most men, as I'm only five-foot-five-inches tall and pretty slim. (I have written elsewhere that I am five foot two inches. This was a misprint. I am petite, but not that small.)

No, the reason the girl had guessed correctly that it was usually I who did the "jilting," to use her vocabulary, was because of my work. These days, the job came first and men second, no doubt in part because I had not so far found the man for whom I was looking. Quite likely, I didn't know exactly what it was that I *was* looking for. In any event, despite a series of enjoyable affairs, I was still single, still living under my married name, still the same Lady Jane Hildreth. I myself very rarely used the title given to me by my former husband, but this reticence didn't seem to affect other people, who I found went out of their way to refer to me as "Lady" and, if they were trying to sell me something, invariably "yer Ladyship."

"Did he give you any warning?" I asked.

"Who?" She seemed to have gone into a temporary trance.

"Your IRA friend. Did he warn you that he wanted to break it all off?"

"Of course he bloody well didn't. I wouldn't have killed for him if he had, would I?"

"Who did you kill?" The question finally had to be put, though I was not surprised when it received no response at all. Instead, she leaned her forehead sideways against the jutting-out part of a headrest and stared out of the window.

Outside, a convoy of motor boats was cutting its way upstream through the flat waters of the Thames, the beautiful, winding, rural beginnings of the great waterway. The boats were presumably making their way back to an evening resting place. On their foredecks, brown bodies lay stretched out to catch the last rays of the evening sun. In the sterns, men with pipes slouched under soft squashy hats behind wheels and beside tillers.

The view of the river soon gave way to the tops of chimneys and redbrick buildings, the most notable of which was the prison where Oscar Wilde wrote "The Ballad of Reading Gaol." I wondered whether the girl opposite had noticed the high, modern outer wall with all its electronic gadgetry, which clashed architecturally with the cold nineteenth-century symmetry of the prison building itself. The train screamed through Reading station; this meant we had only twenty minutes to go before we reached London Paddington.

"I'll give you one clue," she suddenly blurted out. "It's Chinese and no one will ever miss it."

"That's all?"

She had turned toward the window again and didn't even seem to notice my question.

I had no doubt that she had already said enough for me to be able to make a citizen's arrest. The only question I had to decide was whether I ought to do so. On the face of it, a confession to murder certainly merited some further investigation. Even so, I still felt it was all rather implausible. The probability remained that she was acting out a semihysterical fantasy, possibly in reaction to having been given the push by a fast-talking Irishman while he languished in jail. It is certainly not unknown for lonely and impressionable ladies to fall for men behind bars. In fact, the syndrome is pretty well established. The women find in these relationships a way of loving that suits them. For them, love without sex has certain positive advantages. They give their love and their pity, satisfy their urge to possess a man, without having to be at the receiving end of the brutishness that in the past has been the price they often have had to pay for too much physical involvement.

Such a relationship was one perfectly plausible explanation for what the girl opposite had been trying to describe to me. It was equally possible, of course, that what really lay behind it all was a criminal liaison with the prisoner. I needed to establish a much more definite reference either on the girl herself or on her convict friend. Without being able to attach a name to one of them, it was going to be very hard to decide what to do about her, whether to give her a word of cheer and wave her on her way or, alternatively, to take her in for a proper interview. If I had a name, I could let her go, knowing that someone would be able to check up on her story later. I chose to restart the conversation as gently as possible. I would at least make one attempt to win back her apparent former willingness to talk freely to me.

"I wonder whether you allowed yourself enough time on your visits," I suggested. "I believe Top Marsden is pretty easygoing about visits. It must all be very rushed for you, coming down for the day on the train like this. You probably had to leave before the end of visiting time, all very upsetting. It can't have helped matters for either of you."

She looked up at me in some surprise. She didn't seem to have expected me to touch on what was a real practical problem, much more mundane and yet also much more relevant in some ways than the grand issues of pride between the sexes or the madness of love. Perhaps she was taken aback, too, by my knowledge of the workings of Top Marsden: the fact that I knew that the prison applied a very liberal policy on visiting, well beyond the bounds of the official guidelines. Visitors to Top Marsden were usually allowed to stay for several hours, especially if they came from long distances. If her friend were really a member of the IRA, she would have had to meet him under special conditions, in a purpose-built room, off the main visiting room and in the presence of a prison officer, but so long as they had not seemed to be passing contraband to each other (virtually impossible to stop in today's "humane" conditions), their meetings would have run much the same course as those in the main visiting room.

The girl's surprise did not turn immediately to distrust. Her first reaction seemed to be one of relief, perhaps that she was able now to talk to someone who clearly had some detailed understanding of what she had been through.

"It wasn't always a rush," she said. "You see, sometimes I used to stay overnight in the area."

"Wasn't that expensive?"

"Not at all. I know a vicar there who runs a church in a place called Little Bisset. It's very close to the prison. He used to give me a bed sometimes; he's part of the visiting service."

And then, abruptly, as if someone had turned off an electric switch, she stopped talking. I wondered afterward whether she had sensed that I was beginning to take too much interest in her. Perhaps she had seen a subconscious look of triumph in my eyes when she mentioned the vicar. It was certainly an important piece of information. At last I had a cross-reference on her. She frowned and stared at the floor as I tried one more probe.

"Did you get on well with the vicar? He sounds a very sympathetic fellow."

"I don't want to talk anymore," she said. "It's enough. Anyway, I want to go to the toilet, if you'll excuse me."

As she stood up, I saw that she was taller than I had expected, with long, athletic legs. I was unhappy about her leaving the compartment at this point, but there was not much I could do about it. I couldn't exactly stop her going to the loo, though I was determined to keep a careful eye on her when she came back. I had decided to take her to Edgware Road police station as soon as we got into Paddington. Hopefully, I would persuade her not to make too much of a fuss about coming with me in a taxi, though I was prepared, if necessary, to call on the station police for assistance. In any event, I would have to explain to her who I was. After that, I would play it by ear.

She had been away for two or three minutes when the train began to slow down as it usually does as it approaches Royal Oak station. There is a complex points and signaling system there for allocating trains to their correct platforms at Paddington.

As the train came almost to a halt, I jumped up from my seat, turned left outside the sliding doors of the compartment, and began to run down the narrow corridor. Something told me I would be too late, and I was right. At the end of the corridor, the main door of the carriage was swinging open on its hinges. I caught a glimpse of her flowing brown hair as she ran along the short platform of Royal Oak station, hitching up her tight denim skirt to give her greater speed. I saw her reach the unmanned exit before the train went round a slight bend and took her out of my sight.

2

As the taxi weaved its way across Hyde Park in the direction of Montpelier Square, I thought about dropping the whole matter. The girl was probably dotty and I had a lot of work on my hands at that particular time, sorting out the remains of an especially messy case. The last thing I wanted was any form of distraction. And yet I had to face the fact that the girl had freely confessed to murder and to a connection with an IRA inmate in Top Marsden. Professionally, the latter was actually of more interest to me. The question, of course, wasn't *whether* I should take any action but what exactly I should do.

When the taxi drew up outside my house, my yellow Georgian front door with its black bone-shaped iron knocker was as welcoming as ever. After paying off the driver, I waited for him to take his cab out of sight around the corner of the square. When I knew he was gone, I went up to the door and pressed gently against the middle right-hand panel. Having in this way temporarily disconnected the alarm system, I turned the key in the lock. Inside the hall, I took a deep breath of the scent of potpourri that came from a large Chinese bowl on a mahogany table halfway down the passage. I tensed slightly as I turned on the light in the hall. The windows and back doors had been heavily bolted, but I had been trained to be very careful when entering any of my properties.

Everything seemed to be in order and I began to climb the stairs toward the half landing. Here I paused to draw back a pair of peach-colored curtains. They were full length and made of heavy velvet and I had to put down my suitcase and pull on them with both hands. As I did so, the whole house began to warm with the last glow of the late summer evening. Through the panes of the French windows, the geraniums radiated a strange luminous light on the patio outside. They looked rather dry and I made a mental note to give them a good watering the next morning. Then I mounted the few remaining stairs to the first landing and my drawing room. I crossed straight over to the far side and again drew back the curtains from the two windows and gazed for a moment into the thick summer foliage dimly rising out of the gardens in the center of the square below. Next, I poured myself a small neat whiskey from the crystal decanter sitting on a mahogany side table. Then, at last, I was able to slip off my shoes and curl my feet under my seat on one of the two sofas in the middle of the room. Warmed by the whiskey and the reflection of the setting sun outside, I gave a sigh and began seriously to plan my next move.

There was no question that it would be the height of irresponsibility on my part not to pass on to the police a description of the Irish girl together with an account of what she had said to me. What would be more difficult would be to accompany this with an adequate assessment of what I thought she had been up to. By the time I had made my decision, the room was dark and my glass was empty. I slid off the sofa and made my way to a low walnut table in a corner of the room. I felt for the switch under a cone-shaped shade of a lamp supported by a rounded rusty-colored china base. As soon as the light came on, I picked up the receiver of the telephone sitting on the table beside the lamp. I dialed a number in Evesham in Worcestershire.

Superintendent John Andrews was apparently watching television when I called. I could make out the excitable voice of a sports commentator exaggerating the highlights of some football match. I had decided to ring John on his home number both because I felt I knew him well enough to do so and because Top Marsden was in his patch.

I had always had a good relationship with John Andrews. He was one of those rare people whose job involves them in constant tension and aggravation but who somehow keeps smiling through it all, not inanely, not totally detached, either, but with some sort of cool sense of balance. His eyes had never lost their twinkle—in my presence at least—however serious the prospect with which they were confronted. I could visualize him now, puffing his pipe from a round, cheerful red face. Although I lived about five miles outside the boundary of his division, as a matter of fact within a completely different police authority (he belonged to Hereford and Worcester and I lived in Gloucestershire), we knew each other quite well. When requested, John would do little favors for me, like arranging for me to have weekend firearms practice when I felt I needed it, I, in turn, kept him in touch from time to time with any innocent gossip I picked up about goings on in the Metropolitan Police, of which we both had once been members and through which we had first met.

"No bodies found in our patch in the last week." The phone seemed to accentuate the chuckle in his voice. "And as far as I know, nothing across the border in Gloucestershire, either. Mind you, that doesn't tell us much, does it? If the girl did kill someone, she could have done it anywhere. It's been very quiet this summer at our nick, Jane, rather different from the London days, eh? Aside the odd drunken tourist, it's all been lecturing to Neighborhood Watch groups about how they can do us out of business by looking after their own property. The boys and girls could do with a bit of action, though personally I hope it doesn't come tomorrow, as I had planned to take a day off and make some use of the fine weather we're having. I had promised to take my cousin George fishing on the Avon, as a matter of fact. He's staying for a week in a caravan outside Broadway."

"What about the girl?" I asked. "How will you begin to track her down?"

"I'll certainly do my best to check up on her story. We'll probably start with the vicar. I know him a bit; comes into the pub occasionally near where I live. Strange fellow."

"In what way strange?"

"He's a bloke with a loud voice, but underneath he's one of those shy, academic types. I find them some of the hardest to get along with. Lives on his own. When he stops by the pub, he sits in a corner by himself. I must say, it's a new one on me that he takes in people for the prison visiting service. I'll find out more about that. I'll also get the office to have a shifty around Top Marsden. Perhaps one of the Assistant Governors will be able to help. Alternatively, we've got pretty good relations with one or two of the senior prison officers. Might be able to pick up something informally from them. Anyway, Jane, thanks for your help. We'll feed everything you've told us into the national system, of course. You're quite right, can't have people running around the countryside confessing to murder without checking up on them; though my guess, like yours, is that she was upset about something or simply a bit round the twist and wanted to grab herself some temporary attention. She probably became scared by the implications of what she had said and thought the easiest thing was to hop it. Dangerous business, jumping off trains, even when they're moving slowly. Anyway, leave it with us, my dear. I'm sure you've got far too much else on your mind to want to trouble yourself further about it. I'll give you a ring if we're likely to need you as a witness or anything."

"Thanks, John, you're a great pal."

"Anything for you, yer Ladyship."

I put the phone down and the matter began to recede from my mind. John Andrews was more accurate than he could possibly have realized. The Evesham police may not have been having a busy summer, but our office had been flat out for months. A number of events had hit us at pretty well the same time. Our department had been brought in to help customs and several police forces around Europe to unearth a truly massive drug racket. The IRA was once again thought to have activated a bomb squad on the mainland and we were meant to be in hot pursuit of this. Under cover of the Intermediate Nuclear Arms Agreement, the Russians were exporting an army of new spies, whom we had to get to know; counterespionage, counterterrorism, countersubversion: So it went on. New initiatives, not to say instructions, seemed to flow daily from the ever-fertile brain of our chief.

The only unsatisfactory part of it all as far as I was concerned was the paperwork. The reason I had originally volunteered for the service was the promise it held of physical action. I have to admit, it wasn't the money that I worked for. Thanks to the generous settlements of my former husband, first at the time of our divorce and then, more surprisingly, in his will (I have written elsewhere about the strange circumstances of his death), I had enough cash to satisfy even my rather high spending habits. I worked for the sheer excitement of it. I cannot claim that I enjoyed it all. I was simply possessed of a driving determination to test and to retest my capacity to stand up to physical danger. It all went back to a childhood phobia, a terror of anything, however insignificant and small, that might hurt me physically. The need as I grew up to overcome this did for me what nannies and cold baths and unkind fathers did for others: It became an unconscious obsession that shaped my life.

The worst part of what I did for a job was undoubtedly the office work, the report writing, the budgeting, the accounting for the use of resources, and, worst of all, the negotiating with other departments for the use of their resources. I didn't exactly resent this side of the work, but it certainly wasn't what had made me give up any idea for the time being of settling down with one man.

I took another sip of my whiskey and thought about the week that lay ahead. As it happened, it was going to be one of those periods of moving from desk to desk and conference room to conference room at headquarters. The thought of this was made lighter for me by the fact that I knew at the end of the week I was due to leave for a long-delayed discussion with some people from the CIA in Washington. This trip would give me an opportunity to visit my New York apartment, which I had not seen for almost six months. There was a highly efficient security service in the block. Nevertheless, I would have liked to have used the flat more frequently than seemed possible at the moment. Apart from anything else, I had some nice things in it, including several quite valuable eighteenth-century English paintings. It would have been good to have been able to enjoy them more. I also knew a handful of quite glamorous men who were near neighbors on Manhattan's Upper East Side.

What was quite certain was that I wouldn't have much time in the coming days to give a lot of thought to the strange young woman I had met on the train. I was glad that my old friend John Andrews had in effect taken over responsibility for her case.

As it was, by Friday morning of that week, I had almost totally forgotten her existence. This was probably as much because I was immersed in a bilateral conference with the chief as that I had simply lost interest in her. Immediately after the meeting with my boss, I planned to catch an afternoon flight to Washington.

I always relished one-to-ones with the chief. He was one of the most consistently attractive men I knew. Perhaps this was because never in my wildest fantasies did I dream of having an affair with him. Now that I think about it, I've always found the remote types the most attractive.

Unavailable he may have been, but cold he was not. His face, it's true, was rather thin, even gaunt, and his receding hairline at first gave him a severe appearance, but his eyes were blue and soft. Rumor amongst the women in the office was that their blueness was the result of years of service in the desert, though I must say I have never discovered the slightest shred of scientific evidence that would suggest physical surroundings can accentuate the color of one's eyes. Be that as it may, the story about the chief's eyes was by now indelibly fixed in the mythology of the office. It was part of the general assumption that he was Lawrence of Arabia reincarnate. For me, it was not their blueness but their twinkle that was the real fascination of his eyes. It ensured that his sharp wit was never cruel, or even unkind, although it was always acute. He spoke in a deceptively quiet voice, which he had once told me he had cultivated during his days with the SAS.

As well as possessing proven physical courage of great magnitude, he had been a Greek scholar at Oxford. The general view was that he was married, but no one at my level seemed to know anything about this part of his life.

On this particular occasion, we were discussing the report I had recently submitted to him on a nasty case of two homosexual senior civil servants who had stupidly opened themselves up to blackmail by the Libyan government. We were on the point of deciding whether or not the officials would be more useful to us if they were left in place when the chief's secretary, the redoubtable Miss Fry, MBE, put her head round the door of his office.

"Superintendent Andrews of the Evesham police is on the phone," she said. "He claims to need to speak urgently to Lady Hildreth. Shall I put him through?" Miss Fry always addressed me by my title and in return I always put MBE on my notes to her.

"Can't it wait?" the chief asked.

"Apparently not, sir."

"In that case, I imagine you'll want to see what it's all about, Jane. Would you like to take the call here? Save you going to your own office."

I nodded. "Thanks. I can't think why he wants me in such a hurry. Evesham's a pretty quiet station."

The buzzer rang on one of the array of telephones ranged along the right-hand side of the chief's large mahogany desk. I walked across the room and picked up the receiver.

"Putting you through to Superintendent Andrews now." Miss Fry addressed me in her NASA-control-type voice. John Andrews sounded rather distant when he came on the line. The tone of his voice was unusually serious.

"I think I'm going to need your help after all, Jane.

· 22 ·

We've found a body, but not, I fear, the one we were looking for."

"A body?" I needed to reorientate myself. For a brief moment, I had genuinely forgotten about our conversation the previous Sunday night. My mind was still weighing up the arguments for and against "turning" a deputy secretary and an assistant secretary and using them to pass information for us to the Libyans. The trouble was that people who have succumbed once to blackmail are notoriously unstable and thus unreliable.

"That's what I said, Jane. The body of a young woman with long brown hair, wearing a denim miniskirt and black woolen sweater. Sound familiar?"

I remained silent, still not properly adjusted to what he was saying.

"The face is almost unidentifiable, mind. It's been cut about with rather a sharp knife, probably the same one that slit her throat."

My mind began to leave the problems of international espionage and return to the memory of last Sunday's train journey. I began slowly to grasp the significance of what he was saying.

"What do you want me to do, John?" I asked. My question failed to interrupt the flow of his thoughts.

"What we can identify of her fits the description of the girl you met on the train. Coincidence, isn't it? We're not sure, mind." John's Worcestershire accent was more pronounced than usual. "As I say, the body's been badly knocked about. That's why we need help with the I.D. Jane, love, I wonder if you'd pop down and give us a hand. I know how busy you are, but it really would be appreciated."

"Pop down when?" I asked weakly.

"We've got her in the morgue in Worcester now. Can

you manage this afternoon? We can send a car to pick you up from Worcester Shrub Hill station and take you back to wherever you want to get to."

"I had wanted to get to Washington, D.C., this afternoon," I said.

"I'm afraid the budget won't quite cover that." I detected the old chuckle crackling faintly down the line.

Over at the other side of the room, the tall, thin figure of the chief was silhouetted against the light from a large Georgian window. His back was turned to me, his mind no doubt working out moves well ahead of whatever immediate decision he was about to make, as he gazed through the trees into St. James's Park. I thought for a moment about the implications of what John Andrews had just told me. It was clear from what he had already said that my presence was crucial for identification purposes. The only question was whether I should try to persuade him to delay matters until I returned from the United States. I knew from experience that however competent the people at the morgue were, the quicker the I.D. was completed, the better. This was especially true when the body had been badly mutilated, as was evidently the case on this occasion.

"Are you still there, Jane?" The voice on the other end of the phone was becoming anxious.

"I think I'd better postpone my trip to the States and spend the weekend in Chipping Campden, John. I'll be on the train that gets into Worcester at about five o'clock. It means changing at Oxford, but the next one doesn't arrive until around seven-thirty. If I caught that one, it would be a bit antisocial for the morgue people."

"I'm very much obliged to you, Jane." His relief was obvious. "This one looks as if it is going to be very tricky. The vicar was no help at all when we went to see him.

Didn't seem to want to know anything about the girl you met. I can't think what's going on there, I'm sure, though, we shall probably have to get back to him. The people at the prison were useless. And now it looks as though your Irish lady's dead and we have no leads to go on at all. Dear, dear, dear. Did I say we were having a quiet time?"

3

There was no scope for any doubt. The corpse laid out on the slab in the morgue in Worcester was quite definitely that of the girl I had met on the train the previous Sunday. The height was identical, so were the clothing, the hair, and the teeth. The texture of the skin and the facial characteristics were impossible to verify, as the head in particular had been appallingly mutilated. Even after it had been cleaned, it was little more than a large scab of congealed blood. Unusually, in a case such as this, there apparently had been no sexual assault. The body had been found by a farm laborer in a cowshed on Fish Hill above the village of Broadway. This was just on the Worcestershire side of the county border and therefore just within the domain of the Evesham police.

As I sat back in the rear of the police patrol car that John Andrews had laid on to drive me back to Chipping Campden, I decided to put my trip to America completely out of my mind for the time being. I owed it to the Irish girl to spend the weekend at least thinking about what might have caused her death. It was possible, of course, that it had been a random act of brutality, but without any signs of sexual assault, this was unlikely. It was more probable that she had already been in deep trouble when I met her and that I hadn't fully recognized her appeal for help for what it was.

I twisted this thought around my conscience as the police car wound its way through a narrow lane, down a gently sloping hill toward Chipping Campden. The view ahead was one of the most beautiful I had found anywhere in the world: rolling fields of ripening corn, the blues of the distant Cotswold hills, and in the foreground the golden greens of the chestnut trees. Above us, a light wisp of mauve was the only suggestion of a cloud.

It came almost as a shock when the driver pulled up outside my cottage. I gazed in contentment for a moment at the lovely old two-story building with the yellow roses climbing around the front door. Built some time toward the end of the sixteenth century in honey-colored Cotswold stone, this was the place I really called home. Inside I visualized the black beams, the inglenook fireplaces, the eighteenth-century mohogany furniture, and the bedrooms done up in pastel shades of pink and green. One room downstairs was almost entirely devoted to the collection of books I had inherited from my father. At the back, there was the garden, with its lawn and chestnut trees and wild honeysuckle.

Somewhat by contrast, on the opposite side of the street, a pair of dungarees tucked into black military boots stuck out from beneath a car, which I noted with some alarm was my own Mercedes. I got out of the police vehicle, thanked the driver, and crossed the road. As I approached my car, I called out in what I have no doubt was rather a pained voice, "What on earth's going on here, Pat?"

The reply was muffled by the underside of my Mercedes.

"Jane? This *is* a surprise. I thought you were meant to be in New York?"

"I'll fill you in about all that in a minute. In the meantime, could I be allowed to know what's going on with my car?"

At this point, the body of the Honorable Patricia Huntington, daughter of the late Earl of Huntington, rolled out in its full oily glory onto the pavement beneath me. She stood up slowly and wiped black liquid from her hands with what looked like a red silk scarf. Her small delicate face, usually white except when she had given it a heavy painting of rouge, had gone pink.

"Pat," I exclaimed with genuine concern, "you're looking very flushed. Is everything all right?"

"It's like this, well, you see." The hesitation was unnatural for her. There was an apologetic look in her normally flashing black eyes. "After I had driven you to the station last Sunday, I distinctly heard a funny knocking under the chassis. So, of course, I decided to have a look."

"And you've been looking ever since." I laughed. "Be honest, Pat, you've been itching to get under that car ever since I replaced it for the BMW."

"That's a bit unfair, Jane. You wouldn't have been very pleased if the thing hadn't been working when you got back from America. As it is, now it's in tip-top shape."

I squeezed her arm, which felt rather frail through the sleeve of the dungarees' tunic.

"As long as *you're* in tip-top shape, nothing matters," I said. I still found it hard to accept that she was in her seventies. I suspected that in a competition shoot, she would still prove to be one of the best marksmen in the service. God knows what I would have done on a number of occasions in the past had it not been for the deadly accuracy of her protective cover.

Her main job these days was to guard my home. She knew that this assignment had been given to her to keep her happy in her retirement and she slightly resented it. She was not above informing me from time to time that the best thing for her health would be for her to be allowed the occasional field trip again. "No need to make me a full-time agent, but a bit of action really would add years to my life."

Nor did I totally discount the idea. One could never be quite certain that there would not come a time when the service might once again need to deploy the formidable skills of the Honorable Patricia Huntington. In the meantime, she spent most of her waking hours tinkering under the bonnets of her remarkable collection of five vintage cars.

"Come over and have a cup of tea," I said. "As usual, I'm badly in need of some good advice from you."

"That sounds fine. I'll just take off these overalls and put on something decent." I smiled to myself. On past precedent, this meant that she would change into another pair of overalls.

"I'll go and open up the house," I said. "No problems since I left?"

She shook her head sadly. "Nope. The last bit of excitement around here was when those Iranian blighters tried to murder you. Do you remember when I made them run round your garden in their underpants with a shotgun up their backsides?"

I remembered only too well. It was the last time, to my knowledge, that shots had been fired in anger in the ancient Cotswold wool town of Chipping Campden. The worst part had been keeping the matter out of the local press.

"What I want to talk about," I said, "is a murder."

She brightened up immediately. "Thank God for small

mercies." She sighed. "I had a feeling this was going to be a better day. I'll be with you in a jiffy."

I watched her enter the front door of her house on the opposite side of the street to my own and then I turned to walk up the narrow path that ran along the right-hand wall of my cottage. At the top of the path, I paused for a moment outside the kitchen door. The hollyhocks and the roses were in full bloom in the garden at the back. Somewhere high above me, probably in one of the chestnut trees, a blackbird whistled to another. Slowly, reluctant to break the summer-afternoon spell, I turned the key in the lock of the door and let myself into the kitchen.

Immediately, the peace was shattered by the piercing scream of my security system. I moved quickly across the kitchen to a little cupboard in the right-hand corner. Its door was unlocked and I felt inside for the small button that would silence the alarm.

With all quiet again. I filled a kettle, put it on the Aga, and sat down at one end of a long, dark oak table. This was the vantage point from which I could survey the full panorama of my beautiful kitchen. At the far end was all the modern gadgetry framed in light oak. The floor was covered in golden brown terra-cotta tiling. From the ceiling hung bunches of dried flowers and herbs. The proudest feature was the gold, blue, and rust patterned plates left to me by my parents. Ranged on three shelves of a seventeenth-century dresser, the fabulous pieces of bone china sent a glowing reflection around the room, just as they had in the past in our home in Hampshire. The eighteen-piece dinner set had always seemed rather grander than its surroundings, although this was perhaps less true today than it had been in the quite, modest country solicitor's home where I had grown up.

Just as the kettle began to steam, there was a light knock on the door and Pat pushed her way in. To my surprise, she was wearing a tight-fitting maroon-colored dress. Now that I could see the full outline of her figure, I noticed that she was looking distinctly thinner than when I had first known her. This was really the one major piece of evidence that she was growing old. Certainly, the prettiness had not totally faded from her face. A ringlet of white hair fell rather seductively across her forehead, and, as usual, her eyes twinkled with charm and intelligence. She must have been an immensely attractive woman when she was young. Not for the first time, I wondered why she had not married; then I thought of my own approach to this issue and the question seemed to answer itself.

I had first met Pat when she had been my firearms instructor on the conversion course I had undergone from the Metropolitan Police to the Special Service. Her reputation as a marksman was well established amongst her students even before we had begun the course. Occasionally, she would confirm everything we had heard about her by performing some dramatic act or other. She had a habit, for instance, when things were becoming boring, of ripping open her jacket, pulling out a side arm from God knows where, and pumping six straight shots between the eyes of a target without seeming to move her body at all. However, it was her kindness and her good spirit that I liked from the start. Happily for me, she seemed to find me quite amusing, too; and so over the years, we had built a friendship that by now would have been hard to shake.

Pat sat down beside me at the kitchen table and quietly sipped the tea I had poured out for her, while I told her what I knew about the naked corpse I had just identified for the police in the morgue in Worcester. When I had finished, she sat in silence for a moment. Then she said, "What a pathetic girl. I don't blame you for putting off your trip to New York. I would have done the same in your place. The IRA connection *is* intriguing, though, isn't it? What's more, it makes your involvement on behalf of the department absolutely legit."

I laughed. "That depends on what the chief says. He may think it's a rather silly distraction. It may surprise you that we have one or two other things going on at the moment. The chief would be perfectly justified in giving them priority."

"But will you ask him, my dear? I presume the department still does Northern Ireland these days?"

"Oh yes, we certainly do *do* Northern Ireland, as you put it, Pat. Sometimes it feels as though we do nothing much else."

"Well, there you are. He'll probably order you to see this one through a bit further. I would if I were him. The new chief seems quite a sensible cove. I'm sure he'll let you delve a bit deeper if you want to. You do *want* to, don't you?"

I poured her a second cup of tea. "Yes," I said decisively. "Even if there wasn't the apparent IRA connection, I would feel under some sort of obligation to find out a little more about the girl I met on the train. I have a feeling that if I had coped differently with her, she might still be alive today."

"I very much doubt that," Pat responded rather sharply, and then asked, "What's the next move?"

"I'll start with the vicar," I said.

"I thought as much."

"John Andrews says he's being tricky. We'll see if a lady's touch makes him more helpful."

"If I were you, I would catch him off guard after one of his services on Sunday."

I nodded. "That's exactly what I'll do."

The next day was Saturday. An hour before lunch, I drove out of Chipping Campden on the back road that leads ultimately to Bidford-on-Avon. After three miles, I turned right, down a windy little road signposted to Little Bisset. When I reached the middle of the village, I parked the Mercedes by a pair of wrought-iron gates set in a high redbrick wall behind which a Georgian house overlooked the road. I locked the car and walked a few yards along the road to a stone wall that ran along the side of a graveyard. In the middle distance, against the backdrop of a perfect blue sky, the red-on-white cross of St. George fluttered proudly from a flagpole above the Norman tower of the parish church. I unlatched a small wooden gate and began to climb a path that wound at a slight incline toward the church door. Almost immediately, I found what I was looking for. On the left of the path, fixed with rusty drawing pins to a rotting notice board, a typed sheet of white paper told me that matins the next day would be taken by the Reverend Thomas Sayers at 11:00 A.M.

Satisfied, I walked back to my car and turned it round a small village green, which I remember being almost totally covered by an enormous chestnut tree. Twenty minutes later, I was back home for the cold salmon salad that Pat had thoughtfully left for me in my fridge. I spent the rest of the afternoon cutting dead heads from the roses and trimming the edges of the lawn. That evening, Pat and I dined at Alexiou's, a Greek restaurant that had, somewhat incongruously, recently opened a few hundred yards down the road from where I lived.

4

I was wakened the next day by the cooing of pigeons in the tulip tree whose branches almost touched my bedroom windowsill. The sun was streaming through a crack in the Laura Ashley curtains. I put my arms behind my head and stretched back on my bed, staring at the ceiling. It was one of those days when it would definitely have been nice to have had a man lying beside me. The fact that there were scores of men around the world who happily would have filled the role and that things were the way they were because I chose them to be so was not much compensation at that particular moment. Perhaps it was time for another try at serious romance. God knows, I had had enough false starts in recent years. I looked at my watch: 9:45. I jumped out of my bed, tripped over my lace dressing gown lying on the floor, and hurried naked through a pair of white louvered doors to the bathroom.

I arrived at the church at Little Bisset five minutes before the service was due to start. Several other members of the congregation were already in their places. A murmur of conversation quieted noticeably as I entered the nave through a Norman arch whose rounded pillars seemed to be sloping so far away from each other that they looked as though they might split their burden apart at any minute.

I sat myself in a pew to the right of the aisle at the back of the church. As I did so, I was aware that several pairs of eyes made furtive glances in my direction. I couldn't say I blamed them for their curiosity. It could not have been every day that a rather pretty woman (I suppose one has to admit it) in her mid-thirties joined this village congregation, unaccompanied and unannounced. Even my dress must have caused some excitement. I seem to remember I was wearing a tight-fitting peach-colored summer suit from Belville Sassoon, at that time one of my favorite designers. It was not entirely an accident that I was looking so conspicuous. Often in my work, you have to operate incognito, at least with the lowest possible profile. On this occasion, I felt it might be helpful to be noticed. Questions would be asked about what I was doing in the village and someone might come forward with unsolicited information about the Irish girl's visits to the village; this might be critical if the vicar continued to be uncooperative.

When he emerged from a small vestry at the back of the church, at exactly eleven o'clock, the vicar was rather a surprise. He was a big man (for some reason, I had expected him to be slight and rather emaciated). His face was covered with a thick red beard, which made him look like a cross between a rugby player and a Shakespearean actor. He marched down the aisle at a pace that seemed to create a whirlwind around him and had the effect of almost blowing us to our feet. The little old lady playing the organ in the rear left-hand corner of the church noticeably increased her tempo as he passed her. She wore a felt hat with what looked like a pheasant feather sticking out of it. By the time the vicar had reached the empty choir stalls, the hat had fallen halfway down her face and this no doubt partly explained the erratic quality of her playing.

The vicar's voice matched his physique. The explosive sound that he made when he announced the first hymn seemed to startle even the regular churchgoers. I assumed they were all regulars, with the exception, that is, of a couple of what looked like teenagers who giggled throughout the service until the marriage banns were read out, when they lapsed into a ghostly hush. Immediately to my left, on the opposite side of the aisle, sat the verger, whose black gown was too short for him (he must have been over six-feet-two-inches tall) and whose stoop added to a rather sinister, crowlike appearance.

The bulk of the congregation sat toward the front of the church on the other side of the cross aisle, which led out to a great studded door on the right. A large middle-aged lady took up a pew to herself at the very front on the left. Dressed in a loose-fitting pea-green cotton dress with a yellow shawl around her shoulders, she seemed from where I was sitting to be singing as lustily as the vicar. From time to time, she would turn round and look in my direction. Her face was round and slightly weather-beaten and without makeup. It was difficult to tell much else about her features except that her gray hair fell over her face in large, apparently uncombed locks.

Opposite her on the other side of the aisle sat a man of similar age. He, too, glanced round at me from time to time. This gave me the chance to make out a round red face protruding from an open-necked shirt with short sleeves. He seemed to know the service by heart and didn't appear to need to use a hymnbook.

Behind him sat a youngish woman who looked from the back as if she might be in her mid-thirties. She had short fair hair and a slim figure that she showed off to good effect in a tight-fitting cotton dress with a small printed pattern of maroon on cream. I couldn't see her face but she carried herself with a confident poise, which indicated that she was likely to be attractive.

Sitting several pews farther back were a man and a woman, each dressed impeccably in a dark suit. Hers was well tailored, with puffed shoulders tapering to a narrow waist and a tight skirt fitting elegantly around her neat bottom. The material of his suit was darker than hers, with a very thin pinstripe. The cuffs of a cream-colored shirt were well displayed below the jacket sleeves. The woman's hair, which was chestnut brown and as shiny as a conker, was swept back behind her head and kept in place there by a tiny black hat. The man's hair was also immaculately brushed down. During the hymns, they both stood erect, shoulders back and hymnbooks held high in front of their faces. From behind, they made a striking pair.

Very much by way of contrast, the couple who were sitting not far in front of me and to my left made rather a shabby sight. The man was tall and gangling; long strands of white hair fell symmetrically all round his head, forming a curtain in front of his eyes. He did not make much effort to join in the singing. His partner was short and very fat and seemed to be bowlegged. She wore a skirt of dirty blue material that looked as though it was held up by elastic above her very big behind. On top, she wore a cream blouse, which rather clashed with the man's linen jacket. Her straight brown hair was cut short, about two inches above her collar. She wore glasses and sang off-key in a loud falsetto. During the responses, she had a habit of being about two words behind the rest of us.

The service itself was unremarkable (standard Church of England matins without any frilly bits) until we reached the point, three-quarters of the way through, when the vicar positioned himself before us in the pulpit. The sermon that followed should not have been memorable. It was certainly humorless and highly theological. He spoke, I would have thought, well above the heads of most of his listeners, about the need for reconciliation between the doctrines of grace and of predestination, good works and original sin.

Two things made this talk extraordinary. The first was the manner of its delivery and the second was the way in which it was received by most of the congregation. I had grown accustomed to the loudness of his voice, but the vehemence and the passion of his speech did come as a new surprise. What was especially odd was that the more obscure the point he was making, the shriller his voice became. There was a bizarre relationship between the level of the tediousness of the argument and the extent of the near-hysteria with which it was made.

As angels on the heads of pins became hopelessly jumbled up, in my mind at least, with God-fearing Calvinistic saints marching side by side with Bunyan and the Pope, the vicar suddenly took out a handkerchief and sneezed. This gave us all a pause for thought and I was able to wonder not only at this strange performance but at the even stranger attention it was receiving. With the exception of the young couple, who began to cuddle each other, and the verger, who filed his nails, everyone in his audience seemed to be mesmerized by the priest.

The large woman on her own, the man with the open-necked shirt, the girl in the tight dress, the smart couple, the tall man and his fat lady, all sat with their faces transfixed toward the pulpit. There was no slouching, no fiddling with prayer books or staring at the sky through the slit Norman windows. Each sat upright in his place, rigidly directed to where the vicar was standing. Given the mediocrity of what he was saying, I found the whole business very odd indeed. At the time, I put it down to some shared religious experience they must all have had, presumably with the vicar in the lead. There certainly had to be some explanation other than his oratory for the hold that the Reverend Thomas Sayers had over these parishioners. As the service drew to a close, I became even more intrigued by the imminent prospect of meeting the man. When he had given the blessing, I assumed that he would move from the altar to stand, as is normal, at the exit from the church to say good-bye to us all as we filed out. Not for the first time, he was to surprise me. What he actually did was to stride down the aisle to the back of the church and disappear out of sight behind the heavy curtain of the small vestry. I waited in vain for him to emerge.

I remained on my knees, pretending to pray as long as I decently could. I was very conscious all the while of the careful inspection being made of me by the villagers as they passed close to my pew. As I began to sit up, I, in turn, had my first good glimpse of the fine aristocratic features of the lady in the dark suit, as well as of the very white face of her companion. I noticed the two of them engage in conversation with the young woman whose appearance turned out to be a little too opaque to be called truly beautiful—pretty, certainly, but not beautiful. I may have been imagining it, but I thought I saw a look of anxiety on her face. She said something to the man that seemed to appeal to him. A smile spread slowly along his thin, pale lips. The young woman did not smile back; nor did the lady whom I took to be his wife.

I wasn't able to get a closer look at the other four members of the congregation, as they had moved outside before I had risen from my knees. I was just able to notice, however, that the fat lady with bowlegs also had a limp.

As I sat up fully in the pew, I sensed that they were all gathering together in the graveyard outside the front door of the church. I imagined that they could well have been intending to accost me as I came out. It would have been quite a natural thing for them to do to a stranger on her own. Who knew, perhaps one of them was planning to invite me back for a glass of sherry.

However awkward it was, I decided to give the vicar a little more time to come out from behind the curtain. I got up and walked a little way up the aisle and stood beneath a patch in the white overhanging walls where plaster had been scraped off to reveal some crude and badly drawn medieval characters. Someone had clearly decided that the quality of drawing was little more than that of the level of graffiti and had brought the plaster scraping to a halt.

As I stared up at the drawings, I suddenly became aware of a tall figure standing behind me. I turned round and looked up into the narrow, suspicious face of the verger. His small eyes struck me as being unnaturally close together.

"What a beautiful church this is," I said in a rather lighter tone than I felt. "Are those medieval murals originals?"

He glanced past me toward the altar, on which two candles were still flickering. When he spoke, it was out of the corner of his mouth and without looking at me directly.

"The vicar knows who you are." He had a slight Worcestershire accent. "He won't talk to you here. If you want to see him, you'll have to go along to the vicarage. It's on the right, about five hundred yards back, down the main road. If you go there now, he'll catch up with you in about five minutes. It's a large red brick house up a short drive, the only Victorian house in the village. You can't miss it. Now, if you'll excuse me, I have to attend to the altar candles."

I nodded to him, despite the fact that my agreement didn't appear to be essential to the arrangements. It seemed to have been taken for granted. When I walked out of the church into the sunlight, there was no one about. All the villagers had disappeared. So much for the glass of sherry.

The verger's directions were accurate and I followed them with ease. I parked the Mercedes in the drive outside what was a rather modest front door for the rambling redbrick building to which it gave entrance. The vicarage was large enough to accommodate several families. It certainly didn't seem very suitable for a single man living on his own. The garden, in particular, looked as if it was proving too much for the present incumbent. The sweeping lawns around the house were cut, but the flower beds were overgrown and the bushes unkempt. I wondered why the church commissioners had not already sold the house, as they had so many similar properties, and put the vicar somewhere smaller and more modern. It must indeed have been one of the few remaining old vicarages still being used for its original purpose. I knew from my father's conveyancing business that these buildings dated back to the days when the priest, together with the doctor, the retired colonel, and the justice of the peace, was a key member of the ruling squirearchy of the village. The architecture of the vicarage had been very precisely designed by the Victorians to accommodate large tea parties and parish get-togethers.

These days, the vicar had become more of an underpaid social worker than a pillar of rural society. His place had been taken by the retired property dealer and the knighted civil servant, and he needed to be housed accordingly. Gone was the requirement for the large bow-windowed drawing room and sweeping croquet lawns. More appropriate now was the office over the garage, the rock garden, and the patio.

Evidently, this transformation had not yet been brought about in the parish of Little Bisset. Here the old order seemed to have survived, albeit perhaps rather temporarily, and rather tattily.

I wandered off the drive onto the grass and stood on a rise in the ground. Below me and on the far side of the house, the Avon twisted peacefully between willow trees and along fields of sleepy cattle, winding its way between Warwick and Tewkesbury. Beyond the river, the view stretched endlessly over the square medieval tower of Evesham church, with Bredon Hill to the left, to the hazy blue line of the Malvern Hills. To their right, a series of faint blobs marked the foothills of the Welsh mountains. It was a glorious view of the still-unspoiled English countryside.

I was on the point of sitting down carefully on a splintered wooden bench when I heard footsteps on the gravel drive behind me. By the time I had turned round, he was almost beside me. Without his surplice and dog collar and dressed in a pair of corduroy trousers and an open-necked dark blue shirt, the vicar looked even more like a member of the Royal Shakespeare Company out for the day from Stratford.

I was standing on higher ground than he was and so was able to look directly into his face, whose dominant feature without any doubt was its thick red hair. This ran from the top of his head, above his eyes, down the sides of his cheeks to a point about three inches beneath his chin. His beard totally disguised his mouth. Beneath the bushes of his eyebrows, his eyes were green and piercing. A faint scar ran down his left cheek just above the hairline. It wasn't a cheerful face, but neither was it an aggressive one. His eyes gave him a slightly fanatical look, though I couldn't be sure that his strange stare wasn't being put on for my benefit. There was, as I say, a theatrical, not quite real quality about him. Perhaps when I came to know him better, I would discover that he was quite genuinely slightly loopy.

I had thought carefully about how I would introduce myself to him and had decided that I would be very direct. This was partly in reaction to the verger's claim that the vicar knew who I was.

"You weren't able to be of any help to the police about the Irish girl," I said, "and now she's dead."

He stroked his beard and nodded. For a moment, I thought he was going to remain silent. Then he spoke with a calmness that came as something of a surprise after his performance in church. His response was as short and as to the point as my opening gambit had been.

"I know," he said. "Her name was Anne."

"Anne who?"

"I only knew her first name."

"Why couldn't you have told this to the police?" My growing irritation was rather understandable.

He shifted his gaze and seemed to stare at something behind me. As he did so, the lids of his eyes opened wider. It was a peculiar mannerism, as I knew that there was nothing behind me that could possibly have attracted his genuine attention.

"Because they didn't ask me and I didn't think it was

important at the time," he replied. "Do you want to come inside?"

"If you think it will be easier to talk there."

He led the way to the small Victorian Gothic-style porch outside the front door of the vicarage. The door itself, half-glazed with cracked stained glass, was open. He appeared to stoop as we entered the gloom of a stone-floored hall. Partly, no doubt, because of the brightness outside, I found it quite hard to see my way. I followed his tall frame as it turned suddenly to the right into a room that was in almost total darkness. Gradually, I began to make out the shape of a large wooden desk, from which I gathered we must be in his study. I remember stumbling over a pile of books and then reaching out for one of the several upright chairs that stood around the room. He sat himself on top of the desk. It seemed natural that I should place myself on one of the chairs opposite and below him. The only light in the room came from the open door behind me and from a tear in a velvet curtain that seemed to be covering a window immediately to my right.

For a moment, we sat in silence. Then he began to speak very quietly, almost mumbling his words from a half-open mouth.

"I didn't know her very well," he said. "In fact, she only stayed here on two occasions. Each time, she came on the advice of the prison visiting people. They seemed to think it would do her good to have a bit of moral support after she had made the visits."

"You told the police that you had no idea who she was seeing at Top Marsden prison."

My eyes were becoming accustomed to the gloom and I could pick out his face more clearly now. As I spoke, he turned his head away from me toward the curtain, which I could now see was hanging by only five of its nine rings.

"That was before I heard that she had been killed." His

voice had fallen almost to a whisper. A shoe slipped off his left foot and clattered to the floor, which I noticed for the first time was completely uncarpeted. I crossed my legs and pulled my dress firmly over my knees.

"She's certainly dead," I said. "I saw her body and it wasn't a very nice sight. Her face in particular was almost unrecognizable."

"I'm sorry," he murmured.

"I imagine it has occurred to you, Vicar, that if you had been more helpful to the police, you might have saved her life." I waited for him to react. When he stayed silent, I continued, "And now all we've left to do is to find her killer. At least you can help us with that."

Suddenly, he seemed to come to life again. Quite unexpectedly, and out of key with the tone of everything he had just been saying, in a voice that was almost as loud as the one he had used in church, he demanded, "Who's 'us'?" "Who are *you*? What the hell's going on?"

"I thought you knew."

At this, he seemed to calm down a little, a new note of weariness creeping into his speech.

"The police told me you had met the girl just before she died and that you were coming to talk to me, that's all." He paused, hoping perhaps that I would take over; then he went on, "They told me nothing about you except to describe your looks, accurately as it turns out, very accurately. They didn't tell me whether you were coming here in some sort of official capacity or whether you were interested simply as a private individual. I realize now that the latter never was very likely, given the advanced billing they gave you. I have the impression that they take you very seriously. Am I right?"

"The local police?"

"Yes."

I decided to be quite candid with him. "I do have a professional interest in aspects of this case, yes."

"'Aspects'? What does that mean?"

"It means that I'm interested in any connections that Anne might have had with the IRA, which spelled out, Vicar, means the Irish Republican Army, some of whose important leaders are currently locked up in Her Majesty's Prison Top Marsden, a place I think you know something about."

I was certain that he flinched at the mention of the three letters—though perhaps it was in response to the new aggressiveness in my voice.

"I wouldn't know anything about that," he replied hurriedly. I decided that this was the moment to give pursuit.

"I am surprised. I thought I understood that you are involved with the visiting service. Surely that takes you over to the prison from time to time?"

"Yes, yes, so what?" He began rather unattractively to comb his thick hair forward with the fingers of his right hand.

"I can't believe that when you're over there you don't pick up some of the prison gossip, especially about the current batch of star inmates. I simply don't believe that you know nothing about the IRA group in Top Marsden. It doesn't make any kind of sense."

He stared at me for a moment. He seemed to be thinking hard as to how to respond to this. When he finally spoke, it was at a much faster pace than before. He began almost to gabble.

"You're right, of course you are. I do meet some of the IRA types from time to time. In fact, it's part of an arrangement I have with the local RC priest. We sometimes do visits on an alternate basis. When I'm over there, I visit some of his people, yes, including the Irish; vice versa, he talks to some of my people when he's there. We've even been known to take each other's services. You may have noticed from the sermon I preached this morning that I believe very positively in the ecumenical movement. It's no great hardship for me to give the sacraments to Catholics. I think Father Braithwaite feels much the same way."

I avoided the temptation of asking him why he had not volunteered all this at the start of our conversation, and contented myself with one question.

"Do you know the name of the man Anne was visiting?"

The question seemed to catch him by surprise, although he must have known it was coming. Perhaps he had been temporarily distracted with his own rhetoric. He looked at me and then sighed and said, "Now that she's dead, it won't be breaking any confidences if I tell you. At least, it won't be breaking confidences with her. Are you sure the body you saw was hers?"

"Yes."

"How can you be certain, if her face had been desecrated?"

I allowed the word *desecrated* to pass and said simply, "Let's just say I have some experience in these matters."

"I see. You don't look the type somehow to be mixed up with these kinds of matters; too genteel somehow, certainly too pretty."

I couldn't be sure as to whether this diversion was contrived or whether he was subconsciously giving himself time to decide how much to tell me. I decided it was time to take the gloves off.

"Mr. Sayers, are you going to give me the man's name? Because if not, we will have to leave immediately for the police station and carry on this conversation there. In that case, I would advise you to bring a toothbrush, as we may well need to continue the talk deep into the night, possibly until tomorrow morning." The effect of this threat was instantaneous.

"His name is Mike O'Flynn. He's done ten years of a twenty-year sentence. I hope you'll leave me alone now."

In the end, it had been relatively easy. The vicar clearly wasn't much of a hero when his back was to the wall. Certainly at this moment, he sounded frightened.

"What was the basis of their relationship, do you know?"

"They loved each other very much. Please will you stop asking questions."

"You mean she loved him?"

"No, it was mutual."

"How can you possibly know that?"

"Dammit, I knew them both well."

"I see," I said. "That's very interesting." I got up and went over to the door and closed it. We were now in almost total darkness.

"Who do you think killed her?" I asked.

I could hear his feet shaking against the side of the desk. I wondered whether the main cause of this trembling was more likely to be fear or anger.

When he spoke, his voice was cold, much deeper than it had been. He sounded as if he was on the verge of hysteria.

"What are you trying to prove?" he asked.

"I'm not quite sure yet," I replied honestly.

"Nothing to do with Hong Kong, is it?" His tone had changed yet again, to a sort of sulky growl.

"It could be," I said quickly, though it was the first time to my knowledge that the Crown Colony had been mentioned in connection with the case.

"Then I really have nothing more to say to you." With that he slid off the desk on which he had been perched for the whole interview and made for the door. He pulled it open with a new urgency and turned hurriedly into the recesses of the house.

I now had more than enough leads to be getting on with and decided not to pursue him for the time being. Instead, I made my own way out into the sunlit driveway.

I drove back through the Cotswold village of Broadway, up Fish Hill, and past the spot where they had found the girl's body. High above me to the left, I could just make out the wooden cowshed half-hidden by a clump of conifers. By the time that I was turning left off the A44 toward Chipping Campden, I had decided not merely to postpone my trip to Washington but for the time being to cancel it altogether. I would ask for immediate permission from the office to make an official visit to Top Marsden.

The case had started with some limited personal interest for me. Anne's death really had, I suppose, touched my conscience. I had a strange feeling that I was at least partially responsible for her murder. Now the matter showed signs of having very wide, possibly international, implications. If these were in any way well founded, the whole business would, as Pat Huntington had suspected, be of a very definite interest to the department for which I worked.

6

Her Majesty's Prison Top Marsden was built in about 1970 at the foot of the Cotswold hills. Its main feature from the outside is an electronically controlled wall that runs round the prison in a square for about a mile. At night, this outer perimeter is floodlit from hundred-foot poles spaced at twenty-yard intervals. The effect is sufficiently startling to make it worth the while of the Royal Air Force to use it for nighttime target exercises.

Inside the complex, there are a series of defensive systems starting with a second perimeter fence and ending with the cell blocks themselves. The locking system is controlled by a central computer that is versatile enough to allow inmates to move out of their cells at night to go to the lavatory. All they have to do is to press a button in their cells; an indicator tells them how long they have to wait, with only one person being permitted to wander around the block at a time. The system will automatically raise the alarm if the man fails to return to his cell by a given time.

The conventional wisdom is that there is only one way of

getting out of Top Marsden before you have done your time and that is by getting yourself a good lawyer. Certainly no one has ever escaped by any more direct means. The high technology of the prison does, however, allow for a degree of freedom for the inmates behind the perimeters. This means that despite the fact the average sentence in Top Marsden is fifteen years, there is a surprisingly informal and superficially relaxed atmosphere between staff and prisoners. There is even a tendency, for instance, for inmates and warders to call each other by Christian names.

The reason I knew all this was that I had paid several visits to the prison over the years to talk to inmates in whom the department was taking a special interest. Since the IRA was one of Top Marsden's *specialités de la maison*, my visits had increased in frequency during recent times. Strangely enough, I had not yet met Mr. O'Flynn, though I certainly knew of him by reputation.

As I parked the Mercedes in the open car park in front of the prison, I reminded myself of some of O'Flynn's basic details: aged fifty-one, completed ten years of a twenty-year sentence for causing several explosions on the mainland and for attempted murder; acquitted of actual murder but nevertheless refused parole on four separate occasions; thought still to hold senior rank in the IRA and no doubt wielding influence amongst the Irish within the prison.

I locked my car carefully and walked the hundred yards or so to the deceptively innocent-looking entrance to the prison. I pushed open a thick glass door and showed my identification card to an officer sitting in a room behind more thick glass to my right. Beside him, four men in light blue uniforms were staring at banks of screens that displayed the layout of the prison.

A voice echoed at me through an intercom system. "The Governor is expecting you, Lady Hildreth. One of my colleagues will take you up immediately if you will step over to the door on your left." I did as he told me and a door made of yet more glass swung open automatically. A uniformed officer was waiting for me on the other side. Without speaking, he led me up a flight of stairs to a landing from which a long passage stretched off to the right. Halfway down the corridor, my guide stopped outside a door to our left. He knocked and entered, apparently without waiting to be told to do so.

The Governor's office was very modestly furnished with a simple desk, two filing cabinets, and one or two upright chairs. A clock on the wall showed five minutes past eleven. A man whom I took to be the Governor rose from behind the desk as I entered the room.

"Good morning, Lady Hildreth. Thanks, George, I'll take care of her now."

His voice was sharp and pointed and with a trace of a northern accent. It rather suited his slight, wiry frame. He was younger than I had expected him to be, probably in his late thirties, one of the new breed of high-fliers in the prison service, no doubt destined at least to become an Under Secretary in the Home Office. He looked at me for a moment uncertainly, as if he was not used to dealing with a woman standing alone in his office. Then he smiled and said, "Let's sit down. Can I get you some coffee?"

I shook my head. "Perhaps later, thank you, Governor."

"Right," he said, still a little awkwardly. "Let's get down to the business at hand, shall we? Someone from your department rang this morning to say you wanted to see O'Flynn. No problem about that from our point of view, no problem at all. But I thought I ought to see you first just to warn you a bit about him. He's an old hand, is O'Flynn. Can be quite tricky. In fact, to be honest, he can be very tricky. As you probably know already, he's been with us for ten years, which needless to say he hasn't appreciated much. That isn't to say that in the normal course of events he gives us much trouble. He's too clever for that. But one thing is certain: He's very tight on questioning. As far as I can tell from the records, he's never given much away at all.

"Your files may show something different. You people sometimes seem to get things out of these fellows which to the layman looks like a load of garbage but which you find useful. One thing I can tell you is that O'Flynn is still important to the IRA. At least, that's our impression, although of course it's not our job to ask people like him anything directly. As a matter of fact, contrary to some impressions, our job is a remarkably limited one here. It boils down to making sure that the inmates stay with us for as long as the judge said they should and that, if possible, they don't go mad, or, worse, burn the place down. It all sounds pretty straightforward, but I'm sure you'll appreciate it keeps us out of mischief." He smiled. "Even causes us the odd headache from time to time."

"I'm interested," I said, "that you think O'Flynn still carries some weight in the IRA. Rather surprising, as he's been out of action for such a long time."

"Well, for a start, we're pretty sure he's their boss inside the prison, and as you probably know, there are quite a few of them here."

"I see."

"I think it would probably be as well if you were to meet him in one of our secure rooms. As I say, he doesn't normally cause trouble, but it's just as well to be careful. That means an officer will be in the room with you during the interview. Is that acceptable?"

I thought about this for a moment and then asked, "Are your men positively vetted?"

"No, I'm afraid not. I don't think the union would like that."

"In that case, I had better see him on my own. Perhaps somebody could hang around outside the door in case the going becomes rough."

He paused and looked at me carefully again. "One of the nightmares of everyone here is that a lady, especially, if I may say so, such an attractive one as you are, might be kidnapped and held hostage. It's a very real worry when you consider that over half the inmate population is made up of convicted murderers, and under new government rules, many of them haven't much chance of getting out, not in the near future, anyway. There's not much to stop many of them killing again."

"If it helps at all," I said, "I have been pretty thoroughly trained in self-defense. What's more, I've had to use it over the years against some rather rough gentlemen, several of whom have been about twice my size. I do see your problem, Governor. It's a difficult one for you. From my point of view, there are, however, two snags about interviewing O'Flynn with an escort. The first is that he might not unbend in quite the way I want him to. The second is that the conversation might proceed down paths that I would not want anyone who had not signed the Official Secrets Act to hear."

The Governor sighed and stared at his desk, whose emptiness seemed to give him no comfort. I couldn't help feeling rather sorry for him. From his point of view, it was an important decision. If I was held hostage, it would, to say the least, not be good for promotion. Finally, he looked up and said, "Very well. Would you like him brought along now?"

"Yes, please. If I may, I'll wait for him in the interview room."

"Sure you won't have that cup of coffee first?"

I smiled and shook my head. "Afterward, perhaps."

At this, the Governor picked up a telephone beside him and issued the necessary instructions.

When O'Flynn entered the room, I was sitting behind a table facing the door. His height, or lack of it, was the first surprise; he looked shorter even than I. His square face was heavily lined and his curly hair was going gray. He must have been a handsome man once. Even now, despite his height and the toll that ten years of prison life had taken, he had a self-assurance that was immediately obvious and that gave him a natural sex appeal.

I had expected to have to speak first, but in fact it was he who opened the conversation; he did so in an accent that was unmistakably from the Irish Republic and not from Ulster.

"I agreed to see you because I understand this is about Anne."

"That's right. You know she's dead?"

"That's what they tell me."

"I saw her body."

"That's what *you* tell me. I assume you're from the police?"

"Sort of," I said.

"Well, you're clearly not from the Undertakers' Association, so you must be British Intelligence. Right? Why the devil have you people stopped calling yourselves MI5 and MI6? It's all Coordination Department here and Special Divisions there nowadays. It's so confusing and such a waste of everybody's time."

He had started to grin but his lips pursed when I asked him, "Did you have her killed?"

He lifted his gaze away from me and stared out of a barred window behind me. Suddenly, his eyes flashed back to me.

They were deep blue and totally without expression.

"Now why should I have done something like that?" he asked.

"Probably because she had served her purpose."

"Which was?"

"To kill for you."

He raised his right eyebrow. "I don't know what you are talking about, lady, and nor, do I suspect, do you."

"She was beginning to talk," I said. "Not surprising, really, after you told her you didn't love her anymore. She was a simple soul, not one of your solid foot soldier types, let alone a fanatic. She just wanted someone to love and to be loved by. Most people are like that. You probably realized that you had misjudged her when it was too late, or maybe you had planned to have her disposed of all along. At any rate, you heard she had been talking and that was the end of it, and, for that matter, of her."

"You're wasting your time," he said. "Go and chase some Russians, or better still, find yourself a good lay. I'd offer my own services, only we're not allowed to do it in here. Anyway, I've probably forgotten how to after all these years. I used to be pretty good, at least that's what they all used to say. Most of them seemed to go away quite satisfied, though to be honest, it didn't bother me one way or the other what they thought. You see, I've always been too busy with the cause."

This was the moment I decided to put the question that was the real reason I had wanted to see him. It had to be asked lightly, almost incidentally. There must be as little hint as possible as to its significance.

"The trouble was, she began to know too much about the Hong Kong connection. She might have gotten away with it without that," I said, smiling at him.

The response was more useful than I could have hoped for. He screwed up his eyes. For the first time, he raised his voice.

"You keep the Chinks out of this," he said, "if you know what's good for you." As I had begun to suspect, the vicar's reference the day before may have been a slip of the tongue but it had had some significance.

I stood up to go and held out my hand to him. "It's been an unexpectedly pleasant meeting, Mr. O'Flynn. If ever you feel you want to talk to me again, please don't hesitate to ask for me. Sometimes I'm in a position to repay any help I receive."

He remained seated, staring at the thumb of his right hand. For a moment, there was total silence in the room. Then he spoke, as if talking to himself. "You may be hearing from one or two of my colleagues." His voice had become so quiet that it was difficult to pick out what he was saying. "Where is it you live, Lady Hildreth, Chipping Campden, isn't it? Not far from here. Nice quiet little town. I had the pleasure once of staying in the King's Arms; excellent pâté before dinner."

I smiled as sweetly as I could at him. "Won't do any good blowing me up," I said. "As I'm sure you'll appreciate, I'm a very small cog in a very big machine."

The moment I had left the prison and was sitting safely in the driving seat of the Mercedes, I called Pat Huntington on the miniature shortwave radio I carried with me. I asked her to put the Chipping Campden house on amber security and to prepare the office to receive a message as soon as I returned home. I knew from experience that despite all the resources and efforts of the authorities, the IRA in Top Marsden was in almost daily contact with the outside world. Mr. O'Flynn's threat needed to be taken as seriously as he had intended it to be.

When I returned to the cottage, Pat Huntington was in cracking form. As I pushed open the kitchen door, she was sitting at the table, dressed in what looked like battle fatigues, fiddling with the knobs of an array of electronic communications equipment in front of her.

"This is more like it." She chortled. "Nothing to beat a good IRA threat to wake us all up." It was as if we were all about to go fox hunting. "Quite like the old days," she went on happily. "I've already moved all that I need into the cottage, of course. Unless you decree it otherwise, I shall stay here for the remainder of the campaign. Just as well, as a matter of fact, because I've already had that wimp of a vicar on the open line. He must have gotten the number from the police, I suppose. They're allowed to give out that number, aren't they?"

"What did the Reverend Thomas Sayers want?" I asked.

"He apologized for what he called his 'behavior' yesterday. He'd like to see you again. Apparently he's remembered something he would like to tell you in person."

I looked at my watch: It was just before one.

"My first priority is to ring the office. Pat, I wonder if you would be kind enough to fix for me to see the vicar this afternoon: place and exact time to suit him."

She left the room, whistling, to use the second phone in the drawing room.

When I met the vicar of Little Bisset that afternoon, all was not quite as it had been when we had last encountered each other. This time, he was dressed in a dark suit and his beard had been trimmed. His office was bathed in sunlight and sprucely tidy. His general demeanor was subdued and hesitant.

"I'm sorry to drag you back like this," he began, "sorry also for the way I acted yesterday. I wasn't quite my usual self, I'm afraid. This whole Anne business seems to have affected me more than I thought."

I decided to match his new mood.

"No problem at all, Vicar," I said sweetly. "As you know, I live pretty close by. When my friend told me that you had something else to pass on to me, I thought the easiest thing would be to come over straightaway."

"Your friend? Oh yes, Miss Huntington. The name is so familiar. Didn't her family own a lot of property around Cirencester at one time?"

"Could have done, but it must have been a long time ago. Pat's in her seventies now. Her parents must have died at least thirty years ago."

"Nevertheless, I'm sure I'm right. Some of my family came from around those parts and I've got a bit of a mind for that sort of information. It hasn't done me much good, though. As you can see, it hasn't gained me much promotion within the Church."

He looked away from me and stared out of the window onto the drive. The glazed look had returned to his eyes. I felt my patience waning.

"You may be right," I said. It was meant to sound brusque. I wanted to get on and return to Chipping Campden as soon as possible. A plan of action was beginning to form itself in my mind and I was becoming impatient to start putting it into practice.

"I'm sure I am." He crossed his ankles and sat back in his chair. As a matter of fact, I think he was right about Pat. I believe the old Earl of Huntington had owned a lot of land in Gloucestershire, although Pat had never brought up the matter with me. Come to think of it, she very rarely referred at all to her life before she joined the service as a young woman during the last world war. At any rate, Pat's early life history was not the subject I wanted to discuss at this particular moment, and certainly not with this rather strange priest.

"I believe you wanted to tell me something more about Anne?" I asked. He passed a hand wearily across his forehead. He seemed visibly to have aged since the day before.

"I remember yesterday saying something in passing about Hong Kong."

"That's quite correct, you did."

"I have thought deeply as to whether I should say anything more to you on this subject. I have concluded that unless I do, you will harass me further, perhaps at a later date. I do not want that. Indeed, I would prefer it if this was the last time we were ever to meet."

"That I cannot promise," I replied hurriedly.

"You must have wondered how I made the connection between the girl Anne and Hong Kong?"

"I assumed it was from something she had said to you."

He shook his head. "No, that's not it. What I failed to tell you on your last visit was that on two occasions she was visited here by a gentleman."

"Can you describe him?"

"Only that he was Chinese and said that he came from Hong Kong."

"And that's all?" My disappointment must have been obvious, although the vicar was now deep in his own thoughts and may not have noticed it. For a moment, he didn't reply. Then, slowly and seeming to choose his words carefully, he said, "Naturally I didn't eavesdrop on their conversations."

"But?"

"But I did by chance on one occasion hear two words that imprinted themselves on my mind."

"And they were?"

"Wo Sing something or other."

"Wo Sing Wo?"

"It's possible." He was wiping his forehead with a handkerchief. I wondered again what was making him so nervous. It was possible that he was leading me on an almighty wild-goose chase. I had to admit to myself that it was just as likely that he knew precisely the significance of the words he had overheard, in which case he might have some cause to be frightened.

Wo Sing Wo was the largest and the most feared of the Hong Kong–based Triad gangs. It had a membership of around 29,000 "soldiers," divided into ten ruthlessly governed units operating around the world and in particular in Britain. In common with its two rival Triad gangs, 14K and Sui Fong, Wo Sing Wo was of relatively recent origin, having been founded in the western districts of Hong Kong earlier in this century. Exploiting the Triad rituals and superstitions, which date back to about the time of Christ (and which originally protected a romantic movement formed against the oppression of tyrant rulers), the Hong Kong Triads had built up a vast and murderous network of extortionists and racketeers, profiting in particular from the growing trade in heroin and other drugs. Their hallmark was the "chop," the revenge attack on rival gangsters or on their own members who had fallen foul of the hierarchy. Because of Britain's historical ties with Hong Kong and because the mainland Chinese have vowed to wipe out the Triads when they take over power in 1997, more and more of the big Triad players were arriving in England. As a consequence of this, members of the department for which I worked were constantly bumping into Triad operations, often, it has to be said, with messy consequences from which my colleagues did not always come off best. One of our most experienced agents had, in fact, been killed only a few weeks earlier on an undercover operation against a new 14K cell that had recently arrived from Holland.

It would be very interesting to know whether the vicar was aware of any of this. I looked at him closely. He was scratching his beard and his eyes refused to meet mine. They seemed now to have fixed themselves on a spot on the floor about two feet in front of my legs.

"The name Wo Sing Wo really means nothing to you?" I prompted.

"No." His response was immediate, almost automatic.

"Then may we talk a little bit more about Anne for a moment?" I asked.

"If we must. That is, if you want to."

"Was she a religious person?"

"What exactly do you mean by that?" He seemed to sense that we were reaching what was for him higher ground. The prospect of a good theological discussion about the meaning of religiosity was perhaps just the distraction for which he was looking.

"Did she go to church?" I asked.

"Yes."

"Your church?"

"Yes." I thought I sensed a defensiveness in his voice, a new note of suspicion.

"Interesting," I said. "She was Catholic, wasn't she?"

For a moment, he didn't answer me. There was complete silence in the room. Then he leaned forward in his chair. His eyes almost exploded with anger. For an instant, I thought he was going to strike me, but his hands remained gripped to the arms of a Victorian carver chair. He began to shout in a voice that was so loud that if the front door was open, it must have been able to be heard down the main street of the village.

"So bloody well what if she was a Catholic? Won't you people ever understand? For the sake of Christ, we've got to crush the church into one. Yes, one bloody church. Does the thought amaze you? He claimed to be God, you know. God. That's one hell of a bloody claim. For a human being to claim that he is God is either a miracle or the act of a total bloody imposter. It's monstrous, monstrous, that those few of us who still believe that He was God should be attacking one another. Yes, damn you, I persuaded Anne to come to my services and you can put that in your bloody police files and keep it there. It will not be a bad memorial to her, not bad at all."

The sweat was pouring down his face. Whatever else he was, he certainly wasn't the wimp that Pat Huntington had called him. I decided it was probably time to try to calm him down.

"It's the fact that she went to your church, not the reasons for it, that interests me," I said. "It means for a start that other members of your congregation will have seen her. Someone might even have struck up some sort of a friendship with her."

He closed his eyes and placed his hands over his face. When he removed them, his anger seemed to have drained away. For the first time during the interview, he looked directly at me.

"I don't think I can help you anymore," he said.

"I certainly don't want to keep you any longer than is absolutely necessary, but there is just one more thing," I said. "I would very much like to have the names of your most regular churchgoers."

He shook his head wearily. It occurred to me that he was older than I had first assumed, probably in his sixties.

"I don't want to help you anymore. I've gone much too far already. They won't like it, my people. They have their own ways." It was as if now he was talking to himself and I was no longer present. "Not everyone understands them. Sometimes I wonder whether I do fully myself."

"You talk about them as a sort of collective, Vicar, as if they had a common identity. Is that true?"

"What?" He seemed startled by my question. "A common identity? Yes, yes. You're obviously a clever woman, Lady Hildreth. No doubt you would have discovered that for yourself. Anne was beginning to get on quite well with them, you know."

"I thought you said she only came here twice?"

"Not quite." There was a new cunning in his voice. "I said she stayed with *me* twice. I said nothing about how many times she came here."

It was clearly of some importance that I meet one or two of the Reverend Sayers's parishioners as soon as possible.

My first call the next day, which was Tuesday, was on Mrs. Shawcross, the well-covered lady who had sat alone in her pew at the front of the church on Sunday. The vicar had finally given me some names and addresses, so I drove straight to her house. This was situated at a rather awkward intersection of roads at the top of the village, so I parked my car about fifty yards away down a lane to the left. "House" is perhaps too grand a description of where she lived. "Cottage" would be more accurate, with pink-washed walls, a thatched roof, and surrounded by a tall privet hedge. It could have been very pretty, but the garden was a mess of dead hollyhocks and other herbaceous flowers strangled with brambles that stretched everywhere, including across a narrow stone path that led for a few yards from the wooden gate up to the front door. When I reached this, it turned out to be divided into two halves, rather like a stable door, with the top half open. I pulled a rusty metal chain and a single bell tinkled somewhere in the dark recesses of the building. Immediately, three black cats and two brown-and-white cocker spaniels rushed in a scrum to the inside base of the door. The dogs started to bark wildly.

The absence of any human response caused me some anxiety. Of all the people Pat Huntington had rung on my behalf, the one person from whom she had found it impossible to elicit a firm appointment had been Mrs. Shawcross. She had not been impolite about it, nor had she produced any excuses. She simply refused to be tied down to any particular time. (I discovered afterward that this may have been because she didn't possess a watch.) Finally, Pat had mentioned that I would arrive at ten o'clock the next morning. On the rather unsatisfactory basis that this had received no negative response, I had turned up at exactly this time. Much to the excitement of the animals, I gave the bellchain a second pull. This time, to my relief, I did hear footsteps at the back. I waited for what seemed like at least a further two minutes and then she appeared.

Her face was almost as round as her body and not unfriendly; it was slightly weather-beaten and as it had been in church, without makeup. With the back of a bare right arm she pushed away some strands of gray hair that had fallen down her forehead. With her left hand, she began to rattle the bolts on the lower half of the door.

"I say, I'm terribly sorry," she boomed. "You must be the lady who was coming to see me about Anne. I'm afraid I've been so busy, I forgot all about you. How rude of me. There, do come in."

She had finally unlocked all parts of the door and the way was free for me to enter. The two dogs jumped at my skirt, one of them laddering my tights. By the time I had struggled free, Mrs. Shawcross had disappeared once more into the blackened interior. I paused for a moment as the cats retreated in front of me and cowered in the far corner of the room. I heard her voice echo from somewhere at the back, "Come on in here. I've got so many pots on the boil. We'll have to talk in the kitchen." I felt my way in almost total darkness out of the small entrance hall down a short passage. The kitchen, when I reached it, was lined on three sides by double rows of bird cages, which were filled variously with canaries, budgerigars, and I think I even saw some lovebirds. The most noticeable feature of the room, however, at least at that moment, was the damp, sweet smell of boiling fruit. A wooden table in the middle of the room was covered with empty jam jars; over on the right-hand side, four large steel pots bubbled on a gas cooker. With sleeves rolled up and sweating profusely, Mrs. Shawcross was stirring one of these with all her might.

"Early strawberries," she shouted. "It's all this good weather we've been having. Couldn't resist picking them. My deep freeze isn't working, so jam is the only answer. I have no doubt I shall give most of it away to the church fête when the time comes."

"I hope not to disturb you for very long," I said.

"Well, what can I tell you?" she asked without looking at me. Before I could answer, she continued, "We all wondered who you were in church, you know. We don't often get anybody quite as glam as you. It quite turned the heads of our menfolk. The colonel has talked about nothing much else ever since."

"The colonel?"

"Colonel Philip Dalrymple. He lives in the Manor House, that's the Georgian-looking place next to the church with the wrought-iron gates. I do hope you'll be going to see him. He'll be most put out if you don't."

"Yes, as a matter of fact, he's next on my list. May I sit down on one of the chairs round the table?"

"Please do. I may ask you to be so kind as to hold a jam jar or two in a moment. It makes it so much easier to get the stuff in without making too much mess if someone holds them steady. Now, where were we? Oh yes, last Sunday. No one guessed you were a policewoman, by the way. Most of us had you down as some kind of a reporter, probably from the *Sun* or *News of the World* or some other frightful piece of trash like that. The colonel thought you were BBC." I thought she shuddered. "Terrible thing about that poor girl's death. I've just read about it in the Gloucestershire *Echo*. *Terrible*. I'm in favor of bringing back hanging for that sort of thing and I find that most of my friends agree with me."

I felt it was time I tried to structure our conversation a little.

"Did you ever meet her?" I asked.

"Oh yes, several times. She used to stay with the vicar."

"But only twice, I understand."

"Did he tell you that?" She faltered for a moment. "Well maybe, yes, only twice."

"I hope you'll forgive me," I said, "I'm becoming a little confused. If you met Anne several times, that suggests more than twice to me."

"Yes, well, she may have stayed with others in the village. I don't know, I haven't got a good memory for these things. You'll have to ask one of the others."

"Who especially?"

"What? You'll have to forgive me; I'm a little deaf these days."

"Who in particular should I ask about Anne? Was there anyone who took her under their wing, who went out of their way to be friendly with her?"

"I think Christine Lewis used to be rather kind to her, but I really don't know."

"The divorced lady with a boyfriend in Hong Kong?"

This much I already knew from a brief telephone call to

Constable Savage, who ran the tiny police outpost in the village (you couldn't really call it a police *station;* it was more a bachelor flat from which the resident policeman covered several neighboring villages in addition to Little Bisset). Constable Savage was a local man and reverted to being an ordinary citizen of the village as soon as he went off duty. Like everyone else, he seemed to pick up his gossip either from one of the two pubs at each end of the main street or else from Mr. Grace at the one village shop beside the green.

Mrs. Shawcross stopped stirring her pot and looked straight at me. Her heavy eyebrows closed for a moment in a frown.

"Yes, I suppose that's the one way of describing Christine," she said. There was a note of irritation in her voice that had not been present before. "You seem to know a fair bit about us already, Lady Hildreth. Were you born with the title, by the way?"

"No," I said, "it was given to me by my former husband."

"We all thought that was it. It all ties up now. Lord John Hildreth of Greysham Park, wasn't it? I seem to remember him dying in rather sad circumstances." Her tone was almost aggressive now. It was as though she was trying to punch her way out of a corner. I decided to respond in kind.

"Mrs. Shawcross, perhaps we could return to the question of just how frequently Anne visited the village. You say Mrs. Lewis used to see a bit of her. What about the Carvers?"

Mrs. Shawcross deliberately turned off the four knobs of her cooker. Immediately, the hissing from the pots began to subside. She crossed the kitchen to an old-fashioned rectangular ceramic sink and ran a stream of cold water over her hands. She dried them on the sides of her ample cotton dress, on whose flowing pattern small dark spots immediately appeared. For a moment, she stared out of a large window at the end of the room, onto what looked like an old orchard of unpruned fruit trees stretching downhill far into the distance. Then she came to the center of the kitchen and sat herself on the opposite side of the table from me.

"Let's get one thing straight," she said. "I hardly knew the girl at all. I didn't even know her surname. As a matter of fact, I don't think she was ever known as anything other than Anne. She came over here once or twice, I think at the vicar's suggestion, to exercise my horse. Apparently she liked riding and had done quite a bit of it back home in Ireland. I've got a horse that needs more exercise than I can give her these days. So naturally, I was delighted for Anne to take her out as often as she was able, which, as I have just said, wasn't very often. There are fewer young people in the village these days. I can't think where they've all gone. I don't get the help with the horse that I used to, so I'm grateful for anyone who knows anything at all about animals to take her out. Anne did just that on one or two occasions; besides that, I really didn't have very much to do with the girl, though she seemed a nice enough kid. There, is that everything you wanted to know?"

"Almost," I said. I was interested in how defensive she had become. "How long have you lived in Little Bisset, Mrs. Shawcross?"

"Seven years. We came here just before my husband died."

"I hope you won't mind my asking, but what made you choose this part of the world for your retirement?"

She looked at me closely before replying. Her firm features must at one time have made her rather a handsome woman. Now there was a leatheriness about her skin and a cragginess about her face, which I imagined represented a sad degeneration of her former appearance.

"Friends," she said. "We came here because we had friends."

"From Hong Kong?" I asked. The question seemed to surprise her. She looked away and said nothing.

"Your husband was a senior civil servant in Hong Kong, wasn't he?" Pat Huntington's telephone researches, using some of her old cronies in Whitehall, were already paying off.

"Yes, he was," she said.

A definite pattern to the village collective was beginning to emerge.

9

My next call was at the Manor House. The black wrought-iron gates were wide open when I reached them. It was as if my arrival was in some way unexpected. I drove straight through into a freshly graveled drive that turned rather awkwardly in a full circle some way away from the house. Having parked my car as near as I could to the front door, I walked the twenty yards or so up a flagstone path. Just before I reached the whitewashed facade of the building, I paused for a moment between two rose beds. All the flowers were of the same color. I had never before seen quite such a subtle shade of golden orange. The buds were mostly closed. Nevertheless, their scent was overpowering and exquisite. I took a deep breath and reluctantly moved on toward the white Georgian entrance. When I pressed the bell, the door was immediately opened. Facing me was a man I had last seen in church forty-eight hours earlier. On that occasion, he had been dressed in a dark suit. Now he was wearing a pair of gray flannel trousers and a fawn cashmere sweater. I remember noticing that the toes of his black lace-up shoes glistened like two small mirrors.

"Hello," he said. "I'm Philip Dalrymple and you must be Jane Hildreth. Daphne has just phoned to say you were on your way."

"Daphne?"

"Daphne Shawcross. You've just come from her."

"Ah, yes. How thoughtful of her. And good of you to be waiting for me like this, Colonel."

"Can we make it Philip?" he asked. "I left the army some years ago and I've been doing my damnedest to break all the old formalities. Do come in, we can't go on talking on the doorstep like this."

Despite his evident efforts to suppress it, his military manner was very apparent. We entered an elegant square-shaped hall with a polished stone floor. Colonel Dalrymple closed the front door behind me with some force and made a firm gesture toward a room on the right.

"Let's go into the drawing room." He said this as though it was an order which he seemed to feel the need to justify. "It's brighter than my study and more comfortable, too."

It was certainly a very pretty room. Two sofas, covered in off-white silk, faced each other like sentinels in front of an ornate marble fireplace. On the far side of the room, a round antique chess table filled the space created by a wide bay window overlooking the drive. Through the window in the far distance, beyond a yellow flowering laburnum tree, I could make out the lush green of the graveyard sloping gently upward toward the porch of the church.

The colonel pointed to the sofa to the right of the fireplace. "Make yourself comfortable over there," he said, pulling up a high-backed chair for himself. "Can I get you a cup of coffee or perhaps something stronger?"

"It's very kind of you, but no thank you. I don't actually expect to keep you very long."

"I see." He seemed surprised.

"There is one thing that would help to speed matters along considerably," I said.

"And what's that?"

"If I could interview you and Mrs. Dalrymple together. She is here, isn't she?"

"Ah, yes." He strode over to the mantelpiece, where he lifted the lid of a china container and drew out a cigarette. He lit this with a large old-fashioned silver lighter; then he leaned back and stared at the window. He seemed to find it necessary to weigh carefully the implications of my request. At last, he blew the cigarette smoke from his mouth and said, "Yes, Sheila's here. But she's been a little under the weather recently." He paused. I had the feeling that he was choosing his words carefully before he continued. "I don't think she'll be joining us. If it's any consolation to you, I doubt if she would be able to add much to what I may be able to say."

"I think I had better be the judge of that," I said firmly.

He looked at me directly for the first time. Then, as if conceding that for the present at least I held the initiative, he returned—I thought slightly chastened—to the chair he had placed to my left.

"Well, we might as well get on with it, don't you think?" he suggested, with what I felt was rather contrived breeziness. "I gather it's about that poor girl Anne. Wretched business. It may sound rather odd, but we'll miss her around here."

"Did you know her well?" I asked.

"No, I wouldn't say that. My wife fixed it with the vicar to put her up here on a couple of occasions, just to help him out. Being a bachelor, the poor old padre was worried stiff that if she stayed at the vicarage too often, tongues would wag. He was absolutely right, of course. You know what villages are: blasted gossip factories. My neighbors would have accused him of playing hanky-panky with her before you could say Jack Robinson, even though every one of them knew that he was just doing his bit for the prison service."

"I suppose you don't have any idea how often she stayed in the village?" I asked.

"Haven't a clue, I'm afraid."

"Would you be prepared to make a guess?"

"About half a dozen times, I suppose. But that would need checking up. I really don't know."

I needed to press the point. "Do you think she came here often enough to form a real friendship with anyone, the sort where she would feel able to unburden herself a bit?"

At first, I thought he hadn't heard this question. His mind seemed to have moved on to other matters. For a moment, he was silent, then, for the first time, he frowned. The effect of this was slightly to contort his hitherto-unlined classical good looks. The only disappointing feature of these was the paleness and the thinness of his lips. Even when they stretched themselves into a smile, they managed somehow to convey a feeling of weakness. In the past, this would no doubt have been disguised with a mustache. I began to wonder how often a mustache had covered the feeble mouth of a military man.

At last, when I had almost forgotten what my question had been, he said with a strange deliberateness, "No, she had no friends in the village."

"You seem very certain."

"I am certain."

The smoothness of his very white skin and the contrasting blackness of his flat silky hair gave him what I can only call a slightly artificial appearance. It was almost as if he had been made up for the part. He certainly looked a good deal younger than the fifty-two I knew him to be.

"Colonel Dalrymple, your last posting was Hong Kong, wasn't it?" In point of fact, I had already checked this with his army records. "I believe you commanded one of the battalions doing border guard duty there?"

He blew a cloud of smoke away from me to his left. Then suddenly, he leaned forward in his chair and looked straight at me.

"That's quite correct, Lady Hildreth. But I'm damned if I see what that's got to do with the death of the Irish girl, Anne."

"Probably nothing," I admitted.

"There must be some connection in your mind or you wouldn't have asked the question. I'm afraid we army people like to come to the point. Intelligence officers are taught to beat around the bush, the rest of us are not."

I decided to respond to his challenge.

"We've heard that Anne may have had connections with one of the Triad groups based in Hong Kong," I said. "Did you ever come across the Wo Sing Wo?"

He seemed to hesitate for a moment, as if despite his earlier words, he had been taken aback by the directness of my question. Then he said, "Can't say I did, but I may simply have forgotten. It's been almost six years now since I left the place. Triad-bashing was police work. In my experience, the British soldier wasn't really much good with Chinese gangsters. They were too slippery for us, and many of them seemed to be too rich and too well connected. They were definitely best left to the local constabulary. In any case, when I was there, we were kept pretty busy watching the Commies on the other side of the border, usually through a good pair of binoculars, but sometimes from helicopters." He drew hard on his cigarette. His right hand trembled for a moment as his fingers moved to and from his lips. "I understand it's all changed now," he went on. "Nowadays what's left of our soldiery is forced to spend most of its time kissing the arses, if you'll pardon the expression, of the communist Chinese. It used to be so straightforward when we were there. The Reds were the number-one enemy. We actually had rules of engagement that allowed us to shoot at them under certain circumstances. Now it's 1997 this and 1997 that. Did you know that these days, if one of our people picks up a Chink who has crossed the border, far from patting him on the back and offering him a hot bath, the drill now is to clap him in irons before making a phone call to the local friendly communist commander in Kwangtung province to arrange for the poor blighter to be sent straight home. Bloody marvelous, don't you think?"

"Do you often think about Hong Kong?" I asked. "I mean in its present situation."

"Not very much." His mind seemed once more to have become distracted.

"I ask the question because one or two of your fellow villagers seems to have had some association with the colony."

"Yes, I suppose that's true," he conceded grudgingly.

"I wondered whether you ever got together to talk over old times, perhaps even to think about how things might work out for the place in the future?"

"It comes up occasionally, but we're not obsessed about it."

"I imagine you knew the Shawcrosses out there?"
"Yes."

"And the Carvers?"

He rubbed his right eye wearily. "Yes, and the Carvers, and, for that matter, Frank Wates."

"The retired schoolmaster?"
"Yes."

"But not Christine Lewis. She would have been too recent?"

He looked away from me.

"You're right again: not Christine Lewis." He paused and then seemed to feel the need to volunteer some explanation.

"If you're wondering how we all landed up in Little Bisset, I think the Carvers told the Shawcrosses about the village and they told us."

"The Carvers having lived here for some time before you arrived?"

"Yes. Leslie has commuted from here to Cirencester for years."

"That's where he has his import-export business?"

"Yes."

I thought about all this for a moment. From what I knew of the social habits of British army officers and their wives, and in particular of how little they mixed with civilians in postings such as Hong Kong, it didn't all quite add up. However, I decided not to pursue the matter for the moment. Instead, I switched the conversation in a totally different direction.

"Did you find the murdered girl at all attractive?" I asked.

He seemed strangely prepared for this question. His answer was immediate and reactive.

"Good God no."

Then his voice trailed off as his attention was caught by a movement behind my right shoulder. I twisted round instantly in my seat.

"Ah, Sheila," he said. "I thought we had agreed to leave all this to me." His voice had dropped to a mumble.

Mrs. Dalrymple stood by the door. She was even more strikingly beautiful than she had appeared in church two days before. Her dark brown hair was perfectly coiffured around her oval face and down the side of her sensuously long neck. Above her high cheekbones, her eyes lay hidden behind long black eyelashes. She wore a peach-colored blouse and a light gray pleated skirt, which was belted above her tight waist. She stood very straight, in a way that looked as if she had been trained to do so. This gave a grace and elegance to her height, which I judged to be almost six feet. She was thirty-nine years old and, like her husband, looked younger than her age.

Appearing totally to ignore Colonel Dalrymple's introduction, she moved around the sofa on which I was sitting and held out a hand to me. She didn't smile, but her voice had a certain warmth to it.

"Delighted to meet you, Lady Hildreth. If I may say so, you're even prettier than the photos of you in the press make out. Come to think of it, most of them would have been taken at around the time of your husband's death. No wonder you weren't looking your best. It must have been an awful time for you."

"I wasn't married to him when he was murdered," I said.

"I had forgotten that." She sat down beside me, her long black-stockinged legs slanting neatly in parallel toward the floor.

"I heard Philip talking about Hong Kong when I came in," she said. "I thought you had come to pick our brains about poor Anne."

"It is possible that there may be a connection," I said. Mrs. Dalrymple glanced hurriedly at her husband.

"I have told Lady Hildreth there wasn't." There was a new sharpness to his voice. It was as if he was signaling to both of us that the conversation was at an end. What he had said was, of course, not strictly true. It had been I who made some suggestions about the possible Hong Kong connection. He had not so far directly addressed the point at all.

I looked at Mrs. Dalrymple. She was staring at a spot on the carpet beside her feet. I decided that this was not the moment to start asking her questions. Contrary to the view I had held when I had first arrived, I suspected that it might be more productive to see her on her own. I turned to her husband.

"One last question, if I may, Colonel. Do you still write articles for magazines and newspapers about Northern Ireland?"

I detected a new anger in his eyes. "Yes."

10

Little Bisset does not have the well-ordered consistency and neatness of classical Cotswold villages such as Chipping Campden or Broadway. Its mixture of architecture is more typical of Worcestershire or Warwickshire, close to each of whose borders it happens to be. Despite this, it proudly belongs to the county of Gloucestershire and is firmly set in the Cotswold hills. Many of its houses were apparently built in or around the reign of Queen Elizabeth the First; unlike those of neighboring villages, they are not on the whole constructed of rectangular blocks of golden Cotswold stone, but of white plastered stone supported by thick blackened vertical and horizontal wooden struts. Some have roofs made of thatch, and others of tiles held together by layers of ancient moss. Several of the big houses are of more recent design: Georgian, Victorian, and even Edwardian, each one overviewed by the square tower of the Norman church.

It was into this pretty multicolored patchword of housing that I set out, having left the Dalrymples. Turning right outside the Manor House gates, I drove for three or four hundred yards through the center of the village. I passed one or two redbricked Georgian buildings interspersed between black-and-white cottages. Behind the main street, modern houses built of bright red bricks and shiny yellow stones straggled haphazardly up the hillside.

At the outskirts of the village, I turned left into a lane that twisted along a narrow valley. Beside the road, a fast-running stream bubbled and gushed its way impatiently back toward the village. I drove for about a hundred yards to a point just before the road became so narrow as to be passable by only one vehicle at a time. Here I pulled into a lay-by on the left and came to a halt in front of a tiny stone cottage with clusters of yellow and purple hollyhocks standing upright like sentries on guard duty on each side of a front porch. I got out of the Mercedes and took a deep breath of hay-scented country air. High above me, a blackbird whistled angrily, in defense of its territory. I hoped this would not prove to be an omen. I suspected that the next interview was going to be more awkward than the one I had just had with the Dalrymples.

There was no bell, so I knocked hard on the graying oak front door. It was opened after a few moments by a girl wearing tight blue jeans, calf-length leather boots, and a blouse that was unbuttoned sufficiently far down to leave no room for doubt that she had decided to leave off her bra for the day. She held on with some difficulty to what looked like a very powerful black retriever.

"Christine Lewis?" I asked.

"Yes." Her voice was a little husky, as if she had a slight cold or had been drinking.

"I'm Jane Hildreth. I hope you were expecting me."

"A bit odd if I wasn't, after the phone call I had from your friend or assistant or whatever she is. How old is she, by the way? She sounds like a hundred and one."

I was glad that I had turned down Pat Huntington's request that she should be allowed to "come along for the ride." By now, she might have had the girl pinned face-down on the floor with both her arms behind her back.

"She's a little younger than that," I said. "May I come in for a moment?"

"I had assumed that would be the general idea," was the less than totally encouraging response. "You'll have to ignore the mess. I only got back from a trip abroad two days ago and I haven't had time to get straight yet."

I saw what she meant when I entered a small, badly lit, low-beamed room that seemed to double up as hall and sitting room. Three suitcases lay on the floor to the right, opened and evidently half-unpacked. When my eyes had accustomed themselves to the darkness, I could make out several pairs of tights overflowing from one and what looked like a light-colored raincoat from another.

"Do you mind if I sit down?" I asked.

"Help yourself."

I chose one of the easy chairs that were ranged around an inglenook fireplace. She sat herself facing me on the other side of the hearth.

"Have you been somewhere nice?" As I asked the question, I wondered whether she would realize that it was not as innocent as it sounded. If she did appreciate its significance, she gave no sign of doing so. She replied without hesitation, "Hong Kong. I don't know whether that counts as somewhere nice these days. In fact, I'm damn sure it doesn't."

"Oh?"

"You obviously haven't been there lately. The place is on the verge of revolution. The Chinese are not best pleased, to say the least, about what we have laid in store for them for 1997, and the expats are worried stiff about what to do with themselves when it's all over. I have a boyfriend in the police out there. He does nothing else these days except teach teenage Chinese recruits how to beat the hell out of their elder brothers and sisters when they go rioting on the streets. Poor little sods. They join the police force for a few weeks and then disappear as soon as Desmond—that's my boyfriend—has taught them how to wield a nightstick. I can't say I blame them. It must be terrifying facing down an angry mob of people who have nowhere else on earth to go. There were a million of them swirling round the racecourse last week. But I'm starting to prattle. You didn't come here to talk about Hong Kong."

"As a matter of fact, I did."

A sudden look of suspicion crossed her face. There was a sulky edge to her voice when she said, "I thought the conversation was going to be about Anne, the girl who was murdered."

"It is," I conceded, "but as I'm sure you know, Anne had connections with some Hong Kong Chinese. I wanted to begin by asking you, if I may, whether you ever met any of them when she was staying with you?"

She ran the fingers of her right hand through the long strands of her golden hair and shifted her bottom back in her seat. Her bright orange lipstick made her face look anemic. A crash course in makeup would have done wonders for her. She needed somehow to accentuate her pale blue eyes, which were overpowered from beneath by her lips and from above by the over-blackened line of her eyebrows. The total effect was harsh and unbalanced, whereas she ought to have been rather pretty.

"She only stayed here once," she said.

I decided to try to match her rather tough manner.

"Sorry to be a bore, but that wasn't quite what I asked."

"No," she said, "I never saw her with any Chinese friends. What a strange idea, though; come to think of it, there are plenty of them around these days. It won't be too long now, I suppose, before Little Bisset has its Chinese take-away. Some of them are quite good-looking."

"The Chinese?"

"Yes."

At this curiously superfluous thought, she seemed to relax a little. "Anne was Irish, you know," she said gratuitously.

"I do know," I replied, and immediately tried to exploit the opening she had given me. "And she had an Irish boyfriend in Top Marsden prison. Did she ever talk about him?"

There was a silence for a moment while she seemed to consider the question. When she spoke again, her voice was softer, somehow more measured than it had been before.

"No, not much. That is, beyond the stuff you would expect from someone in her position. Of course, she wanted me to know that she thought the guy was innocent and that she would wait for him to come out. I seem to remember there was a bit of chat about his next parole review."

"That conversation must have taken place sometime before she was killed."

"Why?"

"I don't think she trusted him at the time of her death."

She thought about this and then said, "The last time she was here was about six weeks ago."

"Really, that recently? Did she ever tell you what her man was in for?"

"No." Her response this time was quick and firm, surprisingly so.

"Mrs. Lewis—it is Mrs. Lewis, isn't it? You do use your former married name?"

She nodded.

"Did you like Anne?"

She got up from her chair. "Would you like a drink?" she asked. "I'm desperate for one."

"No, thanks, but don't let me stop you."

"You won't do that, I assure you."

She crossed the room to a black oak chest standing against the wall behind me, and lifted its lid. Turning round in my seat, I could see that the chest was filled with several lines of bottles. She selected one of these and stretched up to a small corner cupboard, from which she extracted a tumbler. She half-filled this with what appeared to be whiskey and returned to her chair.

"I don't know what you mean by 'liked,'" she said. "She was rough, not really my type. But, in common with several other people in the village, some of whom you have already met, I felt sorry for her."

"Just that? Sorry?"

"Yes. She was a human being with a problem. I find I can relate to people like that these days. I am much better with them now than I am with the success-story types. I can't cope with them anymore. I suppose I prefer to feel sorry for someone than to be felt sorry for."

"Your boyfriend, is he a success-story type?"

"Would you stay in Hong Kong if you were successful? They're all there now because they've got nowhere better to go for the next seven years. After that, God knows what happens to them."

"You worry about him a lot?"

She took a large drink from her glass.

"I worry about me and him a lot, if that's what you mean. I have some money from my former husband, but that wouldn't go very far if I had to keep Desmond and me in bread. As it is, a good deal of it is disappearing into the coffers of British Airways and Cathay Pacific, care of whom I trot backward and forward across Europe and most of Asia to see him."

"You pay for all the trips yourself? That's well over a thousand pounds return. A lot of money."

She did not answer my question directly.

"There's no way Desmond could do it. It's rather typical of my luck that I should meet a penniless policeman from Hong Kong on the rebound from the breakdown of my marriage. But there it is. We're not allowed to pick and choose with our emotions. You take what's on offer, ride the tide, or whatever is the appropriate cliché."

I sensed she was becoming sufficiently unguarded for me to be able to focus on the subject I had decided several hours previously was the main reason for my visit.

"Where did you meet him?" I asked.

"In a pub in Dublin, if you must know. He was home on leave and I had gone there to drown my sorrows."

"He comes from Dublin?"

"For his sins."

I was not too concerned for the present about what this implied. I assumed that it meant that Dublin had failed to provide him with the right openings and that this had forced him into exile in Hong Kong. My immediate priority was to meet the man himself and if possible to persuade this lady to make the necessary arrangements.

"I'm going to have to visit Hong Kong myself in the near future," I began.

"On the trail of Anne's Chinamen?"

"Partly."

"Why are you telling me this?" The coldness had returned to her voice.

"I was wondering whether I might perhaps be of some help to your Desmond. If he's interested, and more importantly, if he's any good, it's just possible that I might be able to suggest some ideas for work over here. We police try to stick together where it's possible."

She raised her glass to her eye level and squinted at me

through its rim. When she lowered it again, her face was expressionless. Her eyes stared blankly in my direction. Then she said very quietly, "You're a bit of a busybody, Miss Hildreth. No, I've remembered, it's Lady Hildreth, isn't it? Well, your Ladyship, you're not going to meet my policeman with my help; I tell you that for free. You're too bloody good-looking for one thing, and you're too bloody nosy for another."

That was that. I could only hope that there were not too many Irish policemen in Hong Kong calling themselves Desmond.

11

Christine Lewis was the only villager actually to be rude to me. My next two, final visits did not provoke discourtesy; they did, however, confirm my impression that some sort of common front had been prepared against my questioning. No identifiable obstacles were being placed in my way, but there did seem to be a general determination not to fall over backward to be helpful. What's more, I had a growing sense that what was being held back from me was likely to be of greater interest than what was being offered.

This was certainly true of my visit to Mr. Frank Wates, the retired headmaster who lived in a new bungalow at the back of the village, beside a rather ugly flat-roofed building that turned out to be the village hall. Mr. Wates was larger and more powerfully built than he had appeared to be in church. His round red face should have made him a rather jolly fellow. The problem was his eyes. These were too narrow and set rather too close to each other for his face to be a happy one. They seemed to be fixed in a permanent unfocused stare. The effect was of someone who was either acutely shy or, if one was being less charitable, who was acutely shifty. I later discovered that he had exceptionally good eyesight, having been a crack rifle marksman. This was despite the fact that he never served in a line regiment.

Mr. Wates lived on his own. His single-bedroomed house was furnished like a newly done-up two-star hotel, or perhaps a headmaster's office in a modern comprehensive school, or even an anteroom in a refurbished army mess: chairs of light-colored wood with hard semisloping backs, two tall, outmoded lampstands, and a print of an elephant by David Shepherd hanging over a small white-painted mantelpiece. The most notable feature of the sitting room was a large multicolored rug, which it turned out he had knitted himself.

I already knew that his last job had been running an English primary school in Hong Kong and that before that he had been a regular soldier with the Army Education Corps. However, I was curious to find out more about his relationship with some of the other villagers, in particular with the Dalrymples. Clearly, they had the army connection in common, although knowing a little about the hierarchies and the tribal loyalties of the various units of the British Army, I assumed that Colonel Dalrymple's membership in the Irish Guards and Wates's in a mere service corps must have cramped the style of any social relationship they may have had. Mr. Wates was characteristically vague on that point.

"We met occasionally at the Yacht Club and the races, that sort of thing. The army connection was coincidental. Anyway, I had left the service by the time that Philip and Sheila went to Hong Kong. I was much closer to Daphne and Bill Shawcross. It was they who suggested that I join them in retirement in Little Bisset, though Bill died just before we moved here. I still miss him greatly; so, I know, does Daphne, though she tries to hide it by keeping herself so busy."

"And who was it who introduced you to the Irish girl—Anne?" I asked.

For a moment, he appeared startled. He pulled his large frame upright in his seat and turned his gaze onto the football field outside the window. I was not sure whether it had been the actual question that seemed to have shaken him or the suddenness with which I had put it. Eventually, he said in what was almost a whisper, "I never met her. I don't even know what her surname was." When he switched his eyes back toward me, they seemed to have grown wider and there was anger in them.

The absence of a surname for Anne was becoming a cause for genuine frustration. I had already exhausted most of the obvious sources of information, such as the visitors' log at Top Marsden. The only discovery I made there was that she had entered a different name on each visit. The changing-shift patterns had meant that this had gone unnoticed by the authorities.

Certainly the Carvers, when I called on them in their small redbrick Georgian house on the main street, were unable to help on this matter. Mrs. Carver was shorter and more bowlegged than I remembered her and he was slightly taller and sparer. Together, they made an odd couple, especially when they began to speak. Mr. Carver muttered almost inaudibly and she had a tendency to shout in a voice that was as high-pitched as I can remember hearing either before or since. Apparently Mr. Carver still ran a modest trading company whose main source of imports was, inevitably, Hong Kong. They had lived in the village for ten years, which made them the longest-serving inhabitants of all those in whom I had an interest.

The room in which we held our discussion was what we would have described when I was at school as "a tip"; that is to say, it was a mess. Old newspapers and correspondence of various kinds littered the floor. An oval-shaped table in the center was laden with several open cardboard filing boxes. There were dirty teacups on two side tables. The only form of carpeting in what was apparently the main reception room was a small off-white Oriental rug, which was spotted with dark stains. The rest of the flooring was bare boards.

Mr. Carver explained the presence in the village of so many former residents of Hong Kong as "a coincidence, no more and no less." I pressed him on this point, as it did not entirely tally with what Colonel Dalrymple had told me. Mr. Carver thought for a moment when I put to him the colonel's suggestion that the Carvers had first introduced the Shawcrosses to the village and that the others had followed in chain reaction. Then he mumbled what sounded like a repetition of his previous assertion that the presence of all the former colonists was the product of one enormous fluke. For her part, Mrs. Carver seemed to become rather agitated by this bit of conversation; so much so that in the middle of it, she got up and hobbled out of the room. She returned a few minutes later carrying three chipped mugs of tea, which in the case of the one that was handed to me was, I'm afraid, left untouched. I wondered momentarily whether Mr. Carver ran his business as untidily as he and his wife ran their home.

As to substantive matters, in line with my previous encounters in the village, I learned very little that was new to me, except for the fact that the name of Carver's trading agent in Hong Kong was Whiting. I was given this information in return for having declared my intention to go on a buying spree when I next visited the colony.

As Mr. Carver closed his front door behind me, I noticed that his wife was staring out at me from one of the side windows. Her long gray hair and her white shirt, buttoned to the neck, gave her an almost ghostlike appearance. I looked at my watch: 12:40 P.M. It was time to return to Chipping Campden and lunch.

The sun was blazing down on my Mercedes as it stood in the road outside the Carvers' house. When I turned the handle of the driver's door, it was almost too hot to touch. I got into the car and pulled back the sunroof. As I drove out of the village and headed westward into the green coolness of the valley below, I came to three simple conclusions: First, I was still a long way from discovering the real relationship between the murdered girl and the villagers I had met. Secondly, ditto about their relationships with each other. Thirdly, somewhere within the unlikely connection between a sleepy little village in the Cotswolds and an outrageously dynamic Oriental city careering to the end of its political and cultural life lay the answer to why Anne had been killed.

Out of all those whom I had met that morning, the person who had most sharply personified this strange geographical link had been Colonel Dalrymple. For a man who had apparently spent the last six years of his life quietly caring for the Manor House in the village of Little Bisset, he was extraordinarily knowledgeable about what was going on in Hong Kong. As he had shown me to the door, and out of earshot of his wife, he had gone out of his way to give me a further appreciation of how things were in the city of his former military command, especially the state of Chinese unrest there.

"It was always nonsense to give them false hope about the democratic potential of the Basic Law," he had said. "Now the chickens are coming home to roost, and how. I wouldn't like to be in charge of keeping the top on the pot now, not with six million Chinese boiling over underneath. They'll have to call in the Red Army before hand-over day; just watch this space."

There was no question in my mind that my next move must be to visit the colony. I judged that O'Flynn's outburst when I had interviewed him in Top Marsden would be enough for the chief to agree with me. Certainly Pat Huntington was very supportive of the idea when we discussed it over lunch in Chipping Campden. She even managed to invent a Chinese proverb to match the occasion, and a rather belligerent one at that: "If you want to kill wasps, always be sure to pour hot water on the nest."

"I'm not quite sure I see what that means in this context," I said.

She winked. "It means you must take me along as an old kettle."

"Ah, now it all fits into place. Let's see what the chief says first."

She scowled. "It's always the same. Once you get up to London, I just become the guard dog again. I'll be dead before you all decide that I'm fit once more for front-line work. Then you'll be sorry."

"I certainly will," I conceded.

The chief's view, as always, was dispassionate, farsighted, and highly practical. "If Wo Sing Wo is up to new tricks, we had better know about it asap. Yes, by all means, Jane, take the next flight out if you wish. As a matter of fact, it's about time we took another look at our network in Hong Kong. There is no doubt the pace is hotting up over there. There's certainly been an increase in WSW traffic in the past few weeks; so much so that we decided a few days ago to pull in one or two of their little fish in London. Not that we got much out of them, but it's good for their high command to know that we haven't lost interest in them. All the signs are that they are still keeping their bases out of this country. No doubt they'll try to move their heavy stuff over here as the end gets near. It would certainly be nice to know if there are any signs of advance parties planning to arrive soon. The one thing we do know, of course, is that in anticipation of taking over in 1997, the mainland Chinese have already laid down detailed plans for instantly rounding up anyone with Triad connections, however loose. The objective will be to shoot the most important of them with a pistol in the back of the neck the moment the Union Jack has hit the ground. What is significant from our point of view is that the Triads know this, as well. The only question is whether the leaders will gamble on being able to buy off what is a pretty corrupt communist leadership, or whether they will cut and run for bases in the West. See if you can get any closer to the answer."

"I'll go and book my flight straightaway," I said.

12

Far below me, Hong Kong Island sparkled in the intense light of the late afternoon. Its rows of skyscrapers pricked upward like little shiny pins. All around them, the purples and deep blues of the South China Sea stretched away as far as the eye could see, eventually to blend with the mountains of the mainland into a haze of lilac. As befitted the busiest port in the world, the sea-lanes were speckled with tiny dots of white foam marking out the positions of a multitude of tankers and passenger liners and junks. The aeroplane twisted to the right for a moment and exposed the olive greens and the darker shades of Lantau Island. Suddenly, without warning, the nose fell forward and we began to lunge down toward the shanty houses of the Kowloon peninsula. A minute later, there was a screech of brakes and we came to a halt at the end of the runway a few yards from the water's edge.

I snapped my briefcase shut and looked at my watch. We were ten minutes early. I wondered whether Simon Carey would have been able to make the airport in time to meet me. When I had telephoned him from the office, he had promised to "do his best."

"The problem is," he had explained, "that I'm doing a spell as one of the Governor's ADCs. That means I'm not really in command of my own movements. In the past, they gave the job to someone with a more junior rank to mine, but it's all become so fraught here that they've upgraded it to a major."

I was looking forward to seeing Simon again. He was, after all, the first male other than my father I ever kissed. Growing up with him gave me the first emotional shock to the system; not the painful, passionate sort I experienced with my husband, just that which comes with the first taste of love. As teenagers, we lived in next-door villages in Hampshire. My father was a country solicitor, and Simon's owned two thousand acres of prime farmland. Simon was my partner in the local tennis tournaments; because he was so athletic, we invariably won our matches. But it was his wavy long blond hair and his wiry good looks that made me the envy of the other girls. Throughout our mid-teens we somehow managed to stick together at dances.

When he learned to drive, we spent a lot of time holding hands at the back of cinemas. There were even the beginnings of what today would be called heavy petting. Gradually, it all began to wind down. This was mainly because we each left home in different directions. He was commissioned into his father's regiment, the Coldstream Guards, and I went to Oxford.

We never completely lost touch, however. He was the first man I had dinner with after my divorce. I was very upset at the time and he disappeared abroad soon after (rumor had it, with the SAS). It had not been the right moment to begin a new romance.

As I cleared customs, I calculated with some amazement

that it must have been over four years since I had last seen him. I began suddenly to feel a little nervous. Strange that, with his looks, he had never married. He was waiting for me as I came out of the customs area. His physical appearance certainly hadn't changed: tall, lean, fair-haired, smiling blue eyes. On the outside at least, it was the same old Simon. He kissed me rather awkwardly on the cheek.

"What a super surprise this is," he said, and he sounded as if he meant it. "You certainly don't seem the worse for wear, old thing. Being a single woman must suit you." I found his dated vocabulary rather charming.

"I'm getting used to it," I said. "And why aren't you married yet?"

"Waiting for you." This temporarily killed the conversation. It was hard to tell whether he was being even a touch serious. He picked up my bags and we walked side by side toward the exit. As the glass doors slid apart, I felt the shock of the humid heat outside. Simon led the way toward a black staff car that was drawn up at the curbside. A chauffeur in white uniform and red epaulets broke off a conversation with a policeman standing beside a motor-bike propped up in front of the car. Simon seemed to feel the need for an explanation. "One of the perks of working for the Governor," he muttered out of the side of his mouth, "is that you get the use of the Government House car pool; and with it these days goes a friendly police escort. You'll probably see in a minute why we need it."

The driver opened the rear door without changing his expression of total blankness, and then stood to attention. The policeman placed his visor over his face and saluted. Simon returned the salute and handed my bags to the driver.

"We'll take Lady Hildreth to her hotel first," he said. As far as I could make out, the driver didn't answer him.

As soon as we were seated in the back of the car, the motorcycle escort waved his right arm forward and we began to move out of the airport. Simon took off his sharp-peaked guardsman's cap and adjusted the leather strap that went diagonally across his chest. He stretched out his legs, which were deeply tanned, at least from below the edge of his light khaki shorts.

He put a hand on my arm. "By gum, it's good to see you," he said. "We don't get many pretty single English girls in these parts these days. And anyway, it's been far too long." He paused for a moment and then said, "Now let's think about this evening. The question is, how tired are you? It's a hell of a long flight, especially as I believe you had to stop in Bombay. Some sort of bomb scare, I gather. Most of the flights come straight through these days."

"I'm feeling fine at the moment," I said. "One of my few great qualities is that I can sleep on aeroplanes, though perhaps not if I'd known we were about to be blown up. I was in a real bomb scare once. It was a bit upsetting. We even managed to find the wretched thing. The only trouble was, we were halfway across the Atlantic before we managed to get it pinpointed, but that's a story for a rainy evening."

"As always, I'm most impressed," he said, looking at his watch. "Look, if you're really feeling okay, I suggest I give you an hour to unpack and have a good scrub in your hotel. Then I'll come back and pick you up and take you to Government House. It's only a few minutes from the Furama. The Governor and Mrs. Governor are having a short break at the country residence and I've been left to mind the shop. I'll arrange for us to have a bite to eat at Government House. You haven't told me exactly what you're up to here, but knowing a bit about the line of country you're in, I've put one of the colony's most senior

· 100 ·

policemen on standby to join us for supper. He will give you all the lowdown on what's going on here, and most of it is pretty low, I can tell you."

"Couldn't be better," I lied. I had rather hoped we would be dining together alone.

We sat silently for a moment, comfortable in each other's company. The four-year gap seemed to have left no sense of strangeness between us. Suddenly, he said, "It's beginning to get pretty bloody out here. The Chinese are not best pleased with what we are doing to them. Can't say I blame them entirely. On the other hand, I don't see what else we could have done. Mainland China would have been a big place to have quarreled with from the other side of the world. Not quite like taking on the Argentinians, which I did have the pleasure of doing a few years ago."

To confirm what he had said, a group of Chinese suddenly broke away from a meeting they were holding on the street outside and began to shake their fists at our car. The policeman on the motorcycle in front of us waved his arm and we began to move forward faster.

"God knows what will happen to the policemen and the other minor officials when we go," Simon muttered.

Supper that night was served to us by waiters in crisp white uniforms similar to the one worn by our driver. Three of us sat around a table in a small room off one of the terraces in Government House, the official residence of the Governor of Hong Kong. Despite the softness of the evening light and the gentle ripples on the swimming pool beneath us, the talk was nearly all of security and of the troubles that lay ahead.

"The real problem is that we can no longer recruit enough men and women to keep the peace." Bayliss of the Hong Kong police force spoke in a low voice with a Scot-

tish Highland accent. Although it was meant to be a social occasion, he sat upright, occasionally twitching his
short gray mustache. He must have been in his early
fifties, but he looked older. His eyes were tired and there
were lines across and down his face, one of which I discovered later was a scar. His words were measured.

"I have the tactical unit under my command and that
gives me some sort of paramilitary capability. But they certainly cannot cope with wide-scale rioting on their own.
So more and more frequently, I have to call on the military for help. The trouble is, they're not as strong as they
used to be. I gather the cuts in the Gurkha Brigade are
still to go ahead?"

He looked at Simon, who stared glumly at the table-
cloth in front of him.

"If the going gets really bad," Bayliss continued, "we
may still have to call on the Fifth Airborne Brigade in
Aldershot. I only hope the RAF will be able to get them
here on time if we need them. The fact is that at the
moment I can't even guarantee the security of buildings
like the one over there." He pointed out of the window
toward the modernistic and cluttered outline of the Hong
Kong–Shanghai Bank building. "We've already had two
major riots, which we only just managed to control. Several people were shot but not by my men, though I cannot
vouch for what will happen in the future."

"Is that why you've started to recruit Irishmen?" I
asked.

"God, I hope we haven't gone that far." For the first
time, he smiled. It gave a boyish quality to his somewhat
battered but open face.

"The truth is," he added, "that pretty well anyone who
applies to us and who can persuade us that he or she at
least attempted exams in arithmetic and English and
hasn't been convicted in a court of law over the past four

years will get in. You sound as though you have someone particular in mind."

"I do," I admitted, "but all I know about him is that his girlfriend calls him Desmond and that he sometimes takes his holidays back in Dublin."

"It should be pretty easy to track him down, if he exists. Would you like me to try?"

"I should be most grateful," I said.

He looked directly at me. "Simon tells me you're part of the funny stuff in London. I imagine you'll make a formal approach to us if you want any proper help."

"Of course. In the meantime, off the record, may I pick your brains just a little bit more?"

He inclined his head forward. "Be my guest."

"My office is particularly interested in the current state of play amongst the Triads."

"Ah." The corners of his mouth turned downward as he started to gaze out of the window.

"You sound slightly disinterested?"

"Everyone from London always wants to talk about the Triads. Seen from my desk, these days they come very low on the list of our problems. Unlike our information about much of the population here, we know a lot about the Triads. We're on first-name terms with many of their leaders. Frankly, nowadays they spend most of their waking hours on the phone to London, Sydney, or San Francisco, dreaming of ways of getting out of the city. A few of them stir up the rioters in the hope of picking up more protection money from frightened traders. Others try to make wonderful deals in Beijing. The important thing is, we know what makes them tick. I wish I could say the same about all the other six million Chinese. But I'm talking too much. It must be the wine you serve up here, Simon. What exactly is your interest in the Triads, Lady Hildreth?"

Before I had time to answer him, a waiter rushed up to the table and said, "Commander, you're wanted urgently on the telephone, sir."

"What a nice man," I said to Simon when the policeman had left.

"Yes, a dying breed, I fear. The no-nonsense, totally straight, tough-as-old-boots colonial cop. I only wish we had more of them just now."

Commander Bayliss returned almost immediately. Instead of sitting down, he stood beside Simon and spoke to him in a voice that was calm but firm.

"I'd better go. There's another mass rally building up in Victoria Park. Some of the unruly elements seem to be taking over. Our people don't like the feel of it at all. Will you excuse me, Lady Hildreth? Thanks for the supper, Simon laddie. Incidentally, Lady Hildreth, my office has now received formal instructions from London to give you any assistance you may require. May I leave it to you to contact us when it is convenient for you?"

He gave a slight bow and turned away. For a moment, his frame was silhouetted against a window, tall and lean, his hair close-cropped. Then he was gone.

When we were alone, Simon said, "He wasn't exaggerating. Life is going from bad to worse here. We thought things had quieted down after we had wrung yet more assurances out of the mainland Chinese about the protection of democratic rights. But the fact is, people here are as worried about the future as ever. No one trusts the military regime in Beijing, and after the massacres of 1989, who can blame them? I honestly don't know what more we can do. We're being much freer with British passports than we were at one time, but that doesn't help the six million or so who still can't get one."

"I suppose we could stop pulling British troops out just

at the time when we're going to need them most," I suggested.

"Of course, but the pass was sold on that one several years ago. If my memory is right, we announced a three-thousand-man cut in the Gurkha Brigade in 1988. You can't reverse that sort of decision overnight. Inevitably, it has a knock-on effect on manpower availability for Hong Kong, but that's the perspective of a simple soldier; no doubt our politicians had their reasons."

"What about the local force?" I asked.

"The plans to build up the Chinese security service simply aren't working out. I wouldn't want to join if I were Chinese. When they finally get here, the Commies are more than likely to treat them as collaborators. Of course, we do our damnedest to get further assurances about all this from Beijing, and occasionally they give us the right clucking noises. One of the problems is that ever since their troubles last year, they haven't seemed really to know what they want themselves. Makes it bloody awkward trying to do business with them, I can tell you."

I studied the frown that had creased his forehead. I had never seen this serious side of him before and I decided I rather liked it. I suppose I still thought of him as a teenage tennis star or, at best, a captain in the SAS who happened to play rugby for the army. I was finding it a little hard to adjust to him as a full-blown grown-up whose actions might actually affect the course of history. If the team with which he was now working got it wrong, and civil order was to break down, hundreds—perhaps thousands—of frightened and angry people might lose their lives, as they had in Beijing four years earlier. Only this time, it would be a British-led police force that would be on the firing line.

"It must be like punching at cotton wool in Beijing at the moment," I said.

"Exactly. They're all bluster and totally without self-confidence. That can make them very dangerous. The best thing would be if the present leadership was replaced by something more civilized and rational, but I am not optimistic."

Whilst we had been talking, the sky had blackened outside. It was becoming difficult now to pick out the expression on his face.

"What an extraordinary change in the weather," I said.

"Yes, it looks as though we're in for a heavy storm. You get these extreme changes at this time of the year."

The light was fading so fast that a waiter lit a single candle between us. Its flame reflected in Simon's eyes.

"Mind if I change the subject for a minute?" I asked.

"By all means."

"I wondered whether you would do me a tiny favor."

"Something amusing?"

"Probably not. I wondered whether you would ask around for me about a Colonel Philip Dalrymple. He commanded an Irish Guards battalion out here about six years ago. After that, he left the army rather earlier than might have been expected, certainly than he needed to. I want to know why. His army records don't give any clue. It might help if you were to find out what sort of a bloke he was thought to be by the people he worked with, civilian and military."

Simon was silent for a moment, perhaps disappointed at the drabness of this request. Then he seemed to relax and said, "I'll certainly see what I can do. There is one source I can think of that might be helpful, though six years is rather a long time ago in this place. The name Dalrymple rings a bell. This is all strictly in the line of business, I assume?" He winked and there was an intimacy between us that we had never quite reached before.

"Definitely," I said. "If he was a boyfriend, I would use official sources only." I returned his wink and he smiled.

"Good. It really isn't my line of country to spy on senior officers, even if they have left the service, unless, that is, it's absolutely necessary." Then, with a sudden change to a slower pace, he asked, "Now, can *I* switch to a different subject?"

"By all means." I mimicked him.

"I've managed to grab half a day off tomorrow. It wouldn't do you any harm to take it easy for a morning while you get used to this place. Why don't we take the Star Ferry over to the mainland and have some lunch together, *tout seul?*"

"I can't think of anything I would like to do more." And I meant it.

13

It was a still, clear morning. The water was flat and blue as the crowded little ferry ploughed its way, as it and its predecessors had done for over a century, past junks and small cargo vessels across Victoria Harbor toward the Kowloon peninsula. We sat in the stern and turned to watch the gap widening between the boat and the majestic frontage of Hong Kong Island. Over to our left, the Royal Naval Headquarters, HMS Tamar, otherwise known as the Prince of Wales building, still flew the White Ensign from its rooftop, though the regular British Navy had long since departed. To the right, almost lost in the maze of skyscrapers, was my hotel, the Furama.

The long, soft strands of my fair hair, which I had allowed to grow to below my shoulders, blew behind me in the boat's slipstream. I thought of tying them down with the silk scarf I had packed in my shoulder bag, but decided that I rather liked the feel of their wildness. I would put a brush through them when we reached the restaurant. I undid a button of my apple-green cotton shirt and allowed the sun to warm the lower part of my neck. I was pleased I had decided to wear white trousers. A dress would have been awkward on the boat.

"What a bloody paradox," Simon suddenly muttered beside me. "Three people killed in the riots last night, one of them a nineteen-year-old policewoman, and still the skyscrapers keep going up all over the city. You wouldn't believe that there are only seven years left. Look at those half-finished constructions over to the right. I'm told they are each going to be at least ten floors higher than the Bank of China building. The Reds aren't going to like that one tiny bit. They wanted their building to be the tallest in town forever."

"Perhaps they're not bothered. After all, it will all be theirs soon," I said.

"That's perfectly true. And the amazing thing is that most of the new stuff is being done with Western money."

I turned away from the side of the boat and raised my sunglasses. The civilian clothes Simon was wearing suited him: well-pressed gray flannel trousers, short-sleeved white shirt with a light blue silk scarf tucked inside its collar, dark blue blazer slung over his shoulder. His hair was a lighter color than it had seemed the day before, with a tinge of gray in it. His eyes were sadder and somehow wiser than when I had last looked at them properly. However, the little boyish grin was still there, as were the full, round lips. His teeth were as white and as straight as they had always been, his jaw as firm, cheeks as lean, and his skin as smooth. Well over six feet, he was still a very handsome man.

"It's got into your blood, all this, Simon, hasn't it?"

"If it has, I'm not much different from most of the people who work here. Did you know that three-quarters of the expats are thinking of staying on after 1997? That's quite a thought, isn't it?"

I thought for a moment of the people I knew who had not stayed on and were now living thousands of miles away in a village called Little Bisset. For some reason, it had not suited the civil servant, Shawcross, to remain, nor the schoolmaster, Wates, nor the Dalrymples. Mr. Carver had not found the place sufficiently magnetic to base his operations here.

Simon got up and leaned against the railings of the boat. I wasn't facing him directly but I could feel his gaze on me.

"I hope it doesn't embarrass you to be told," he said, "but you've grown up into a very beautiful woman. John Hildreth was an ass to let you go; the thought of it still appalls me."

"Well, he's dead now," I said, staring hard at the water.

"How long are you planning to stay?" he asked.

"As long as it takes, I suppose. I doubt if I will be able to call on the taxpayers' generosity for much more than three days. I should be able to get everything done in that time."

"That's very quick."

"And how about you? How much longer do you expect to be here, assuming you're not planning to stay on like the other expats?"

He shrugged. "It's all becoming so sensitive. They're beginning to promote anyone who knows the remotest thing about the place. If they think you're going to be any use, everything is done to encourage you to stay on and see the show through. That gives me another seven years or so."

I was rather sorry to hear this.

"By the way," he said, "I've had a quick word around

about your friend Dalrymple. He was certainly here about six years ago. He didn't seem to make much of a mark, which probably means he didn't do anything particularly stupid, ordering a raid over the border or something. Anyway, his memory has faded somewhat into the mist of time, but the old hands say that he was rather a quiet, intellectual type. Apparently he did have some ideas about how we should sort out the troubles in Northern Ireland, but they were thought to be rather cranky and nobody seems to have paid too much attention to them, or, for that matter, to have remembered any of the details. He had a rather pretty wife but she clung to him and the rogue bachelors gave up trying to chase her after a while."

"Thank you," I said.

"Not much help, I'm afraid."

"I'm not so sure."

"One day you must tell me what it was all about."

"Unfortunately, there's nothing much to tell at the moment: a murder; the victim has connections with the IRA and possibly with Wo Sing Wo; the trail leads to a small village in the Cotswolds where several of the retired inhabitants have been tied up in one way and another with Hong Kong. That's about it for the moment. I wish I could tell you more, but try me again in a week or so."

"Sounds much more fun than worrying about what words of comfort the Governor should give Exco the next time he meets them."

He sat down and placed his arm along the railing behind my back. His fingers were long and elegant.

"Remind me what Exco stands for," I said.

"The Executive Council, the Governor's appointed cabinet."

Without our noticing it, the ferry had begun to dock at the Kowloon pier. People were beginning to leave their seats and to jostle toward the disembarkation point.

"That was quick," I said.

"It's only meant to take eight minutes."

We joined the general stampede to leave the boat and then walked for ten minutes along the quay to a tall modern building standing on its own patch of grass. Once inside the large tinted glass doors, we took the lift to the fifth floor. We stepped out into a restaurant filled with roses and pink tablecloths and surrounded with panoramic views of the city. The headwaiter seemed immediately to recognize Simon and led us to a table overlooking the harbor.

"Spicy or sweet food?" Simon asked.

"Spicy."

"Szechuan?"

"I love it."

"I think you'll find it's all pretty good here, better, in fact, than the Grand, the hotel that is supposed to have the best reputation in these parts."

He ordered in Chinese.

"That's impressive," I said. "I had no idea you spoke the language."

"Very limited Cantonese, I'm afraid. It's a swine of a language to learn; even they don't know what half the characters mean."

"You seem to have made a pretty good start. At least the headwaiter understood you."

"It's become rather important for anyone in the government business to know what the Chinese are saying. Unfortunately, the only way is to learn their language."

I was beginning to understand why they would want to keep him on. While we waited for the food, we drank gin and tonics.

"Before I get completely drunk," I said, "can I talk shop just one more time? Then I promise I'll shut up."

"Don't do that. There's so much to catch up on."

"One of the Little Bisset crowd was the headmaster of a primary school out here. I can give you its name. He's called Wates. Before he became a schoolmaster, he was in the army, where he was apparently a champion rifle shot. He's a bachelor and a strong-looking fellow. I would dearly like to know what he got up to in his spare time. Then, if you can bear it, there's a somewhat eccentric widow of a former government official, called Shawcross. I have a feeling that her dead husband is likely to be of more interest to us than she will be. You see, he was Irish. Finally there is Mr. Carver. He should be easy to track down through the British Trade Mission. He's a rather seedy businessman who apparently still comes here quite often. Apparently he uses an agent called Whiting. It's out-of-hours stuff I need, Simon, what they did with themselves when they weren't teaching or running the government or making money."

Simon stared for a moment out of the window. His eye seemed to follow the course of a large passenger ship that was steaming gently from left to right across the harbor. Tiny figures standing on its upper deck were waving furiously at the shore. Then he turned to me and for the first time our eyes met. He seemed to wince at the contact and immediately disengaged. He began to gaze intently at the bowl of roses in front of him. I wondered whether all this was out of shyness or whether there was some other reason.

Suddenly he said, "I'll do my best. I'll need some more details, of course."

The lunch, when it started to arrive, soon became a relay of little dishes, beginning with crispy pancake rolls with spiced duck.

"Can you manage some Maitai?" he asked. I was too busy concentrating on the noodles in a sweet-and-sour soup to answer. The clear liquid was poured into two small glasses. He raised his and said, "To Messrs. Wates and Carver and to Mrs. Shawcross and to Colonel Dalblimple and all who sail with them."

"Dalrymple, silly." I laughed. Then I put my hand over his. Before he could remove it, I said, "To our re-discovered friendship."

Then I lifted my glass and took a sip from it. The taste was sickly and burning.

"What awful stuff," I croaked.

"You get used to it. The Chinese like to drink the whole glass in one swig, like this." He put his head back and poured the entire contents of his glass down his throat. "Now your turn," he said.

"No thanks, I might be sick."

"Okay," he conceded. "Let's share your glass. Let's toast to us and take alternate sips." I laughed and we did as he said. After one or two sips, I was becoming light-headed. I suddenly became aware that the headwaiter was standing beside us. He paused politely while Simon drained off the dregs of his glass. Then he said quietly, "Phone call for you, Major Carey. They say it's urgent."

Simon immediately caught the seriousness in the man's voice. The smile faded from his eyes.

"Sorry, Jane," he said as he rose from the table. "I always have to say where I am even when I'm supposed to be off duty."

I watched his upright form weave its way between the tables and disappear behind a bar on the other side of the room. We were both busy people, very much in control of our emotions. I wondered for a moment whether one of us might let it snap.

When Simon returned, he was frowning. It was the first time I had seen him look genuinely concerned.

"Something big's come up," he said. "I'll have to get back to Government House asap. The Governor will need a full briefing on this. They're sending round a staff car straightaway. It should be here in about five minutes. When it has put me off, it can take you round to your hotel. I'm so sorry to have to mess things up like this."

"Don't worry," I said. "It's been a wonderful morning. Honestly, I've enjoyed every moment of it."

He leaned over the table. This time it was he who squeezed my hand.

"I hope we can do it again before you go."

As we drove down into the Cross Harbor tunnel that links Hong Kong Island with the mainland, I asked him whether I was allowed to know what was going on.

"I don't see why not," Simon said. "It'll probably be all over the television evening news in a few hours' time. The police have apparently uncovered a major arms cache in the monastery on Lantau Island. It's been a nightmarish worry of ours for years that one day the rioting mobs would have access to serious weapons. Well, now it seems they may have. Powerful guns have started to arrive in large batches."

"Any idea where from?" I asked.

"Not yet, but clearly that's one of the first things we shall want to find out."

The car turned left off Harcourt Road by the naval headquarters and began the short, steep climb up Peak Hill. Government House loomed large and ugly to our right. The Japanese had recognized its commanding qualities when they had established it as their control post during their period of occupation. Even today, dwarfed as it was by skyscrapers, it was still a focal point for the city. I imagined I was not the first person to wonder what the communist Chinese would do with it. It seemed hard to believe that they would simply tear it down as a symbolic act of termination of colonial rule. It looked somehow too permanent a fixture. As we approached the main gate, police sentries in khaki shorts and half-sleeved tunics came to attention. The smartness of their flat-handed British Army salute was unlikely to be emulated by their successors.

The car wound left and then right up a short tarmac drive before coming to a halt under the porch that covered the steps leading rather grandly up to the front entrance. Simon patted me on the arm and said, "I'll be in touch as soon as I know what the Governor wants me to do."

He got out of the car and called to the driver through the front window, "Could you please take Lady Hildreth back to the Furama?"

Had it not been so hot, I would have been happy to walk the half mile down the hill to my hotel. As it was, physically and, I suppose, emotionally slightly weary, I was glad of the lift. I waved at Simon as he bounded up the steps and disappeared into the building.

When I arrived back at the hotel, there was an envelope waiting for me at the reception desk. The note inside instructed me to ring the London office immediately. I went straight to my room and dialed the duty officer. When I finally got through, I didn't recognize the voice that came on the line, but his message was straightforward enough: "The chief says that we are also interested in where those arms came from."

I slipped out of my trousers and shirt and turned on the bath taps. I must admit that as I poured oil onto the steaming water, my thoughts were as much about Simon Carey and the few hours I had just spent with him as of the problems of finding the source of some arms find. Once I had sunk fully into the bath, I closed my eyes for a moment and then stretched up my right arm to feel for the telephone on the wall beside me. I dialed the Government House number and asked for Simon Carey.

The girl on the switchboard rang his extension. What seemed like several minutes later, she came back to say that there was no answer. "I'll try 'Secretaries,'" she said. After a few moments, a middle-aged and very upper-class English voice came on the phone.

"Lady Hildreth?"

"Yes."

"Major Carey tried to reach you about ten minutes ago but your line was engaged. I'm afraid he has had to leave town rather urgently and won't be able to be reached until he gets back."

"Leave town?" I repeated, totally nonplussed. "But the whole place is one town. Does that mean he's left Hong Kong?"

"I'm afraid I don't know."

"When do you expect him back?"

"Again, I'm afraid we have no idea."

"What an extraordinary business. I can't believe that you are not in a position to give me some idea of what he's up to."

I thought I heard a sigh at the other end of the phone. "I'm afraid these are unusual times over here. People in Major Carey's position do things without warning. Even we in the office don't always know exactly what is going on. I've worked here for fifteen years and I have never known anything like it. It's probably time I went home and settled down in some quiet little village in the heart of the countryside somewhere. Several of my friends have done just that. Sometimes I feel it would be sensible to go and join them. Incidentally, Major Carey did leave instructions that we were to give you every assistance if there was anything you wanted."

While she had been talking, I had had time to collect my thoughts. The lady was right: These were unusual times in Hong Kong and Simon clearly had a highly sensitive job to get on with. He might, for instance, have had to go to Beijing on the orders of the Governor. It would all be very last-minute stuff and obviously not something he would wish to broadcast too widely. He probably didn't even fully trust the staff in his office; much of it, I gathered, was locally recruited these days. Silly to get strung up about the whole thing. Anyway, I had quite an important job to get on with myself.

Two days ago, Simon Carey had been only a remote memory; one that meant nothing to me at all. And yet, now that he was gone, I realized, without having been conscious of it before, that I had begun to assume his presence as part of my life, at least for the next two or three days. And when I thought about it, two or three days was about the limit of my current planning horizon. For me, it was a long time.

"There *is* something you could do for me," I said to the woman on the phone. "You could put me in touch with Commander Bayliss, the police officer I had supper with last night."

She seemed relieved to change the subject. "Of course; no problem at all. Would you like me to give you his number or do you want me to get him to ring you?"

"I think the best thing would be if you could possibly fix for me to go round and see him later this afternoon."

"I'll certainly do what I can, Lady Hildreth." Then she added, "I am sorry about Major Carey."

I wondered whether she had sensed the nature of my disappointment. The thought went through my mind that it might not have been the first time that she had had to use sympathetic words on his behalf to comfort half-tearful ladies. For a moment, I wanted to prolong the conversation, at least to ask her what her name was. It was too late. The line had gone dead.

It would not really be surprising if he had other female commitments in town.

Commander Bayliss's office was large, semicircular, and
had magnificent views on all sides of Victoria Harbor. It
was a room I would have associated more with a business
tycoon than with a policeman, but then, I was used to
British working conditions for public servants.

We sat beside each other Chinese-fashion, in two large
easy chairs, in a corner facing the windows. Bayliss had
taken off his tie and had undone the top button of his
white sleeveless shirt. His northern Scottish lilt was even
more pronounced than it had seemed to be the night before. His close-cropped hair suited him. It added to the
sense of firmness and efficiency that there was about him.
In full daylight, I could now see that a faint scar ran down
his left cheek. Being with him again now, I felt Simon
had been right to bemoan the passing of his breed of colonial policeman. The world would not necessarily be better
off for the departure of his type. Men like Bayliss had been
tested from Central Africa to the Hindu Kush, and on the
whole I suspected they had served their fellowman well.
They had been hard and inflexible, but because of that,

they also on the whole had been fair and incorruptible, with no pretensions to imposing any single grand design on those whom they policed. They simply took the values that were handed to them and made sure that they were applied smartly and uniformly. Sadly for them, they did not fit easily into retirement back home, where their status was indeterminate and certainly not on a level with the positions they had earned for themselves abroad. Commander Bayliss was the last of a sort. It was hard to decide which pew he would be allocated in the church at Little Bisset or wherever he finally ended his days.

"First things first," he began. "We do have a Desmond O'Grady on our books and he comes from Dublin, at least as far as we can tell. I'm not sure if he's the man you're looking for, but he fits the limited description you have given me. This man does mainly undercover work. Paradoxically, in view of what I said last night, he is one of the few officers still working on the Triads."

"That's very interesting, Commander. I am very grateful to you. It would be nice if we could find out if he has a girlfriend called Christine Lewis who lives in Gloucestershire in England. It would be important that he should not be made aware that I was making these inquiries about him."

"I think we can probably arrange that. What is going to be more difficult in the immediate future is for you to meet him. The problem is that he has just been assigned to this arms-find job on Lantau Island."

"Has he just?" I was becoming more interested by the second.

"You see, we think there may be a Triad connection."

"Any particular gang?"

"Could be Wo Sing Wo. They're probably the only one with an international network capable of handling a job like this. As a matter of fact, we picked up one of their small-time hit men near the scene of the find last night. But your friend O'Grady should be able to establish the facts within the next few days."

"May I ask you, Commander, how you came to uncover the arms?"

The policeman looked at me directly. He was, no doubt, carefully weighing up how much he ought properly to tell me.

"Do you really need to know?" he asked.

"My office is showing an interest in the subject. As I assume you are, they are very concerned about the international ramifications. My side of the department deals almost exclusively with the international perspective, though as I'm sure you know, the service is nothing like as compartmentalized as it used to be."

"Quite right, too." I could see that he had been flattered to be put a little into the picture about the structure of the intelligence service back home. It was a world of which I suspected he knew very little and therefore about which he probably fantasized a lot, whilst at the same time resenting his exclusion from it, and I didn't wholly blame him; it was quite probable that the Russians had a better idea of my job description than he ever would.

"As you know, we made the find in the Buddhist monastery of Po Lin on Lantau," he said. "There's a monk living there called Ho Ceilu, who was in the Hong Kong police force at one time. Need I say more?"

"Has he been brought in for protection?" I asked. "If so, I wouldn't mind seeing him."

The policeman opened a box on the low table in front of him. I shook my head when he offered me a cigarette. He lit his slowly and then said, "There's no question of protection. The monks out on the island are a law unto themselves. Many of them have made great material sacrifices to live out there. Some of them have even cut themselves off from successful business careers to follow Buddha. Nothing in this world would induce them back to the mainland. Some of them, like Mr. Ho, are very welcoming and hospitable to visitors; they even cater for coach tours, for which they provide vegetarian lunches." He made a grimace. "Not my taste at all. But that's the sum of their contact with the outside world. The reason I suspect Ho Ceilu gave us the tip-off had nothing to do with his former connection with the police force. I would guess it was because of his outrage at the intrusion to his way of life that the arms shipment represented. The last thing he would wish for would be further interference from the police, even though he must realize that his life is now in grave danger."

"Do you think there would be any objection to my visiting him?"

"None as far as I am concerned. As I say, he's always been very welcoming to visitors in the past. I might even be able to lay on a police launch for you if you would like it."

"I think that might embarrass Mr. Ho, don't you? Is there a public ferry that goes out there?"

"Yes, there is, but if you take it, I suggest that I arrange for you to be picked up at the landing stage on the island by some form of suitably discreet land transportation. It's a long walk to the monastery from where the ferry will land you."

At this point, there was a knock on the door and a young policeman entered the room. He was dressed in the distinctive light green tunic and shorts of the Hong Kong police force, with a Sam Browne belt running diagonally across his chest. A handgun holster was clipped to the back of the belt around his waist. He approached Commander Bayliss and handed him a note. Then he stepped back a pace, saluted smartly, and retired from the room.

Bayliss's face remained totally expressionless as he read the note.

Then he turned to me and said in a low voice, "Apparently the army experts have been able to establish that the arms have come from Libya. It's very strange. Triads don't usually deal with the Arabs. They simply don't understand or, for that matter, particularly like the ways of Islam. They consider Islamic religious zeal to be at best a mark of collective madness and at worst a sign of dangerous unreliability."

He paused to draw deeply on his cigarette. When he exhaled, he allowed the smoke to drift gently up toward the ceiling.

"This looks like the big one we've all been waiting for," he said. "Or rather, the one we've all been dreading. I don't know how much you've been told, Lady Hildreth, about the nature of the arms haul. The fact is, we picked up a thousand semiautomatic small arms, at least fifty machine guns, not to mention mortars, and enough ammunition to withstand a siege for weeks. In other words, we've found enough weapons to equip a small army. The only question is, how much more is there that we haven't unearthed? There's no doubt about it, some very big fish are behind all this. I doubt if they will have much difficulty in replacing everything we've already discovered. I am sure you understand the full significance of this from a policing point of view. Up till now, we have just about been able to contain the mass rallies and the riots, even the outbursts of violence, sometimes admittedly at the cost of the lives of our officers, as was tragically the case last night. Now I'm not so sure. We certainly can't match a properly armed force, not at least in the way we're trained to do things, with the minimum of bloodshed. Even if we were systematically to shoot to kill with the help of reinforcements from the UK, we couldn't suppress six million people. Anyway, it's unthinkable. I wouldn't stay for five minutes if that became policy. I'm afraid, though, that this arms find could mean Hong Kong is about to fall apart before we've handed the place over. Makes me begin to wonder if the best part of my lifetime has been a total waste of time."

All of a sudden, he looked tired and much older. The room darkened for a moment as the sun went behind a cloud. Then, before I had had time to respond, he changed the subject.

"Simon Carey seems to have left town. You don't happen to know where he's gone, do you?"

"As a matter of fact, I don't," I replied. "We had lunch together. He kindly said he would look into the background of one or two people I'm interested in back home and who have connections with Hong Kong. Our lunch was cut short by the news of the arms find. When I tried to reach him soon after returning to my hotel, he had apparently disappeared without a trace."

"Not entirely without precedent," the policeman said. "He's a very competent fellow and the Governor relies on him more and more for his hush-hush stuff, especially when this involves trips north of the border. Still, it is odd that I haven't been told anything. Sometimes the political boys think it better to keep us on a 'need to know' basis. That way, it's thought we all get on with our respective jobs more efficiently and without tripping over each other. I hope I can track him down within the next twenty-four hours or so. There are one or two matters arising out of this arms find that I really do need to talk over with him. It certainly does put the colony's security into a totally different perspective. I shall obviously need to discuss the matter formally with the Governor, but it would be nice to chat it over with Simon first."

For a moment, he appeared almost to have forgotten my

presence. He seemed to be thinking aloud to himself. Then, recollecting the business immediately at hand, he said, "What's more, it would be far better if we could fix up your visit to Mr. Ho through Simon's office rather than through mine. I entirely agree with your reservations about making your visit look like a police project. With or without Simon, I'll get his secretary to make the arrangements directly with the monastery. Government House is always fixing it for guests of the Governor to go out there. It will look much better that way."

"That sounds fine, Commander. His secretary certainly sounded pretty much on the ball when I talked with her."

"Ah yes, that's Mrs. Longbotham; she's a good lassie."

"She sounded rather older than a lassie to me. Anyway, I'll get out of your way now. I know how busy you are."

"You're right. Gone are the days, I'm afraid, when senior policing was about meeting good friends for a four-hour lunch at the club. It's all work and not much play now."

"You've been very helpful," I said. "If I may, I will take up your kind offer of ground transport on Lantau Island. May we make it early tomorrow morning?"

"I don't see why not, so long as Government House can make the necessary arrangements in time. Incidentally, although we want to keep out of the way as much as possible, I think it would be as well if we were to provide you with protection. The Triads can be pretty nasty and Wo Sing Wo is in many respects the worst of the lot. What's more, I am afraid it's always possible, however careful we've all been, that someone will have tipped them off that you are nosing around their operations."

My mind reflected back to the accuracy of Mike O'Flynn's information about me when I had met him in Top Marsden prison, and I said, "A gun certainly might come in handy, Commander."

"That wasn't exactly what I had in mind," he replied.

"I didn't bring my own out of respect for the independence of your command," I told him.

He still seemed to be doubtful. "I'm sure you understand I shall need to check back about this with your office. If they give their blessing, one of my officers will have a weapon for you when you get off the ferry at Lantau. But please don't kill any Buddhist monks. The last thing we want is trouble with them, though I suppose it may eventually come to that if they've been helping with the arms shipments."

I rose to go. He had anticipated my move and was already standing above me. I held out my hand to him. He looked straight at me, tall and impressive. As we shook hands, I said, "If the handover to the Chinese takes place with any semblance of normality, the population of this colony will owe you a great deal."

I thought afterwards that this must have sounded a little pompous; nevertheless, it was well meant.

15

I leaned over the railings at the side of the ferry and my
eyes traced the coastline of the island we were approaching. They followed down the undulating contours of rich
vegetation and raced sideways along curving lines of white
beaches. Eventually, they came to rest on the cluster of
whitewashed and stilted wooden houses that make up Silvermine Bay, the largest village on Lantau Island. I could
not help being impressed by the remoteness of the place.
Only one hour away by ferry from the roaring metropolis
of Hong Kong, it was as if we were reentering medieval
rural China. No wonder it was such good recruiting
ground for the Triad gangs.

As we approached the small pier, I thought I could
make out the man I was looking for. He was short and
thickset, as he had been described to me. Dressed in an
open-necked white shirt and gray shorts, he stood, with
arms folded, slightly apart from the rest of the small waiting crowd. As soon as the boat docked, he raised his
thumb toward me and I knew that he must be my police
escort.

When I stepped ashore, he hurried forward and put out his right hand.

"Sergeant Li Sing?"

"Yes, ma'am. Welcome to Lantau Island."

"It's very beautiful. I had no idea that Silvermine had such a lovely beach."

He smiled. "Thank you. I was born here. Please come this way. Unless you wish it otherwise, we will go straight to Po Lin monastery."

He led the way toward a small gray van that was standing in the shade about fifty yards back from the water's edge.

"Not very comfortable, I'm afraid," he commented as he opened the passenger door for me.

For a few moments, we drove in silence along a narrow macadam road. Then he shouted above the noise of the engine. "Mr. Ho is expecting you. Apparently he has prepared a small meal for you. I hope you like vegetarian food."

"I'm sure I will. Tell me, Sergeant, have you come across a Constable Desmond O'Grady working on this arms job on the island?"

As there was no reply, I thought he hadn't heard me and I began to repeat the question. He broke in, "I heard the question the first time, ma'am. I'm afraid the answer is yes."

"You don't sound over the moon about him, Sergeant."

"No ma'am, I'm not. I've known him for a year or so and I'm not, as you say, over the moon about him. I don't trust him. He never seems to me to have any commitment to the force." Then he qualified himself. "But then, I suppose that goes for most of the expats these days. You can't blame them; they'll all have to leave in five years' time and most of them have nowhere else to go."

"But Mr. O'Grady is in some way different from the others?"

"Yes."

"Why?"

"How well do you know him?" He seemed to be giving himself time for thought.

"I don't. I have just heard about him. The only information I have about him is that he's from Dublin and has a girlfriend who lives in the heart of the English countryside. I did meet her once."

"He has no friends in the force, but that may be because he is neither British nor Chinese. My own feeling is that there is more to it than that. He's a loner. He never makes any effort to be sociable or even to be polite to his collegues. He works hard, though. I have to give him that. He and I were in the same unit for a while. We worked on anticorruption in the good old days when that was uppermost in our minds. That was real police work, unlike all the paramilitary things we have to do today. These days, they really want us to be soldiers. Any genuine police work is almost something you do on the side."

"You say Mr. O'Grady worked hard when you were close colleagues?"

"Yes, he very rarely left the office before nine o'clock at night."

"No girlfriends in town?"

"Not that I knew of."

"Did he ever talk about Ireland?"

"No, though I sometimes used to have the feeling that he thought about his home a lot."

"It must be strange for him, working in a British colony."

"You mean because he is Irish?"

"Yes," I replied. "The Irish are brought up to despise

and detest the British colonial past, of which they claim themselves to have been victims."

"It is true," Li Sing conceded, "that in my presence he has talked of the "bloody Brits," but I have always put that down to his generally aggressive character."

"Whatever the truth of that matter, he certainly seems to be a strange choice to put onto a job as sensitive as this one," I said, and then added, "Is he here now?"

"On the island, you mean?"

"Yes."

"I think so. In fact, I'm sure he'll be somewhere on the island."

"Perhaps we could try and meet him after we have seen Mr. Ho."

The police sergeant looked sideways at me to make sure I was being serious and then said, "If that's what you really want, ma'am, it shouldn't be too difficult to arrange. I think I know how we can find him."

As he spoke, he wound down his window and pointed upward to the right. "There's the monastery now," he shouted.

We continued to climb steeply for a further five minutes. When we finally reached Po Lin monastery, it turned out to be a rather squat building, but with uninterrupted views across the surrounding valleys toward the South China Sea.

Sergeant Li Sing parked the van in the shadow of the main wall, close to the entrance. When he had switched off the engine, he lit a cigarette.

"You should come here when the sun rises. It is very beautiful," he murmured contentedly. He drew a few puffs on his cigarette. Then he kicked open the door beside him and jumped onto the ground. He walked slowly round the front of the bonnet to my side.

"Is it all right to leave the van here?" I asked him through my window.

He shrugged. "There is nowhere else." Then he opened my door and I saw that he held a gun in his hand. "You requested this," he said.

"Thank you," I replied. "Not quite the way I expected to receive it, though."

"I'm sorry," he said, "I was told to give it to you just before we entered the monastery, but not earlier."

"I believe you," I said. "Now let's get going."

I jumped down from the van and joined him in the heat outside. We began to walk toward a flight of steps that led up to the entrance of the outer temple.

As we reached an archway at the top of the stairs, a figure stepped unexpectedly from behind a pillar. His head was shaven and he wore loose-fitting robes. He approached us with both his arms stretched out before him in greeting.

"Welcome," he said. "You must be Lady Hildreth. We are expecting you." He spoke in a perfectly cultured upper-class English accent. His face was unlined but I put his age at late forties. His eyes possessed a depth and a wisdom that seemed to suggest a wide experience of life.

"Mr. Ho?" I asked.

He nodded.

"It is extremely kind of you to see me at such short notice."

His response to this was somewhat opaque. "All time seems to have become shorter. Perhaps it is as well, because these are not good times."

"I imagine you have some idea why I have come?" I asked.

"Yes, yes." He made a gesture with his hands to indicate a certain impatience with my question. "I hope you and your companion will shortly join me for some refreshment. But first, please allow me to show you a little of our monastery."

For the next half hour, he led the way through several temples, in three of which we stood before the great Buddhas of Po Lin. After this, we were shown the living quarters where the monks spend their waking hours reading and praying in tiny cells and where they sleep at night in open dormitories. Every so often, we passed groups of Mr. Ho's colleagues chanting together. Once or twice, we saw a monk on his own, seemingly lost in the trance of meditation, completely oblivious to our presence. Finally, Mr. Ho led us to the refectory; here bowls of vegetables and cups of green tea had been laid out at the end of one of the long tables. He motioned to me to sit on a simple wooden bench in front of the food. Sergeant Li Sing sat down beside me. Ho handed me two wooden chopsticks and a plate, on which he began to place pieces of vegetable that he picked from the bowls scattered in front of him.

"Can we talk in confidence here?" I asked, glancing round the large room with its many recesses and shadowy corners.

"Of course."

"I believe the weapons were found under a room close to this refectory?" I began.

"That is correct. They were discovered off a room to the right through the door behind you. It is still being guarded by the police. That is why we cannot go and look at it, though I assume, being someone in authority, you would be able to get the necessary permission should you wish to do so, Lady Hildreth."

I did not respond and for a moment he studied me through his shrewd eyes. Then he said, "This business is not good for our monastery. That is why I do not believe that any monk will have had a hand in it, though I know that is not the view of the police. It is because I wanted you to understand it, Lady Hildreth, that I was willing to receive you here today. Nobody in the monastery would have had the slightest motivation to conspire to bring this disaster into our midst."

"Not even out of fear?" I asked.

"Lady Hildreth, we may have cast off the ways of the world here; we may have turned our backs on the hurly-burly of Hong Kong; but we are not fearful men. On the contrary, since we have nothing to protect but our souls, we have nothing to fear. Fear, you know, springs in large measure from greed and selfishness, from a requirement to hold on to physical possessions and from the need to demonstrate ability. We do not have that kind of fear here."

"So the gangs were playing on your innocence?"

He smiled. "Wrong again, I'm afraid. We're not innocent, either. That is to say, we do not go about our lives unaware of the forces at work outside. Most of us, including myself, have at one time or other had very active, not to say complex, lives on the other side of these walls. I know, for instance, that I risk my life talking to you. It is neither innocence nor foolhardiness that prompts me to do so."

"What is it then, Mr. Ho?" I asked.

"The need to cleanse and to protect the name and the life and perhaps the very existence of the monastery. That is all that matters to me and to my brothers."

"Is there anything you particularly wish to tell me?"

"Indeed there is," he said, "but please sample a little more of our cooking first. I know your palate will be finding it hard to take, but I assure you, after a short time you would, as they say, become hooked on our type of food."

I picked up what looked like a small sprig of broccoli and put it in my mouth. As I chewed it, I stared back into now-smiling eyes. The broccoli had what was for me an unpleasantly acidic taste.

"Now I will tell you," he said, "as time is not on our side. I must get to my prayers and you must catch the ferry. It is very wise of you to have brought your friend Mr. Li Sing, whom I take to be a police constable. Am I right?" He laughed merrily when neither of us responded.

Then, quite suddenly, he became serious. "What I have to tell you is known by many villagers all over the island. I did not wish to know it and I do not enjoy passing the information on to you. As I have said, I do so because I love the monastery and because I believe in peace. Lady Hildreth, the authorities believe that the arms were destined for the Triads, to enable them to make trouble as we approach 1997. This may be an accurate deduction. Gangsterism of whatever kind always does better when there is trouble. That, after all, is what racketeering and protectionism is all about. But I am bound to tell you, this business goes much, much deeper. I fear its roots stretch right back to what I believe you call the Emerald Isle."

"Ireland?"

He nodded.

"The IRA?"

"It's a long way from home for them, and I could not tell you what is the precise connection between what the Triads are doing and the operations of the Irish Republican Army, but there is little doubt that the connection is there."

The monk wasn't to know that I had first heard the same suggestion less than a week earlier on the other side of the globe. The emotionally disturbed vicar in Little Bisset, the convicted IRA murderer, and the Buddhist monk from Hong Kong: Were they really part of a single pattern?

"How can there possibly be evidence of this?" I asked. "It is so improbable. What can the IRA want out here?" The questions came out more sternly than I had meant them to.

He shrugged. "I am not knowledgeable about world events these days, but it used to be the case, when I followed these things, that anything that was an embarrassment to the British, especially in one of their military establishments, was good news for the IRA. They've blown up your bases in Germany and had a try at Gibraltar, so why not Hong Kong?"

"So far, the IRA has never worked through proxies," I said. "If they are planning to stage something, they will use their own people, at least on past precedent."

"I think you will find that they have their own operatives over here, even perhaps within the police force, in which as you may know, I was myself once employed."

"Desmond O'Grady?"

"He looked at me steadily for a moment and then said, "It's against the principles of my religion to talk of names. In fact, I am afraid I cannot help you anymore."

He stood up and lifted his right leg to adjust the strap of his sandal. "All I can tell you is that it is common knowledge amongst the villagers that the IRA has been around. What their motives are I must leave you to work out. Now I will lead you back to the main gate, where I will say good-bye."

The sun blazed down on our heads out of a purple-blue sky as Mr. Ho led us across two courtyards toward the entrance arch. He was silent now. I assumed he must be preparing himself for his prayers. He walked with an athletic firmness. The sun reflected itself on the crown of his shaven head, which he held high and with evident pride. Lean and upright, he was my idea of a godly man.

As we came out of the monastery, I noticed with some relief that Li Sing's van was still standing where he had parked it. Mr. Ho bowed to me as I climbed into the passenger seat. The police sergeant had already placed himself behind the steering wheel. He fumbled in the breast pocket of his tunic for the ignition key. I closed the door on my side and felt behind my right shoulder for the safety strap.

Suddenly, I heard a crack of a rifle shot. Mr. Ho, who was standing outside, about two yards away from the van, looked up in surprise. A bullet hole appeared in his forehead. His eyes rolled upward toward the heavens. Blood began to flow from the corners of his mouth as he fell on his back.

I drew my gun from the folds of my skirt and threw myself from the vehicle.

"Get out," I shouted at Li Sing. "It's probably booby-trapped."

With some presence of mind, the policeman rolled over to the side of the van that I had just left, and fell out onto the ground beside me. Our backs were now against the wall of the monastery. The van was placed between us and the vegetation on the other side of the road, from where the shot that had killed Ho had undoubtedly been fired.

Li Sing began to work on a miniature radio set that he had somehow conjured up from his person. Within the space of a few minutes, several police emerged from the monastery, where they had presumably been on duty at the place of the arms find. They moved cautiously toward the dead body. Then they raised it gently and carried it back to the building from which a moment earlier the monk had emerged with such natural dignity and, as it had turned out, with so much courage.

"We must find Desmond O'Grady," I said to Li Sing.

"We have to drive to a fishing village called Tai O," he said. "It's on the northern side of the island; it will take about twenty minutes to drive there."

"We'd better borrow a police car," I said. "There must be one around, with all this activity going on. We certainly can't use the van until it's been cleared for explosives. Could you get a message through to whoever's in charge here telling them what we plan to do?"

As Li Sing had suggested, it took us less than half an hour by police Land-Rover to reach the little riverside port where Police Constable O'Grady was said to have based himself. We drove straight to the village police post; from there, we were directed to a small white painted house overlooking the river. A policeman from the post accompanied us as we raced the Land-Rover to the quayside and came to a sudden halt in front of a three-story house from which most of the plaster seemed to have peeled away. The room that O'Grady was using was apparently on the first floor and could be reached from the front of the house by means of an iron staircase that led up onto a wooden balcony. O'Grady's room was the first on the left at the top of the stairway.

We ran up the single flight of stairs with our handguns primed. When we reached O'Grady's door, the two policemen crashed themselves against it. Inside the small darkened room, there was no sign of the Irishman. There was, however, plenty of evidence to suggest that someone had left the place in a hurry. Drawers had been left half-open; the bed was unmade; books and papers were scattered across the floor.

"I suppose that probably means he's left the island," I suggested.

Li Sing nodded. "He may even have got out of Hong Kong altogether. It just depends on how much time he has had."

"Not much, judging by the mess he's left the place in," I said. "He must have done a runner, as they say in the Metropolitan Police force, as soon as he heard about Ho's murder, unless, that is, he's just naturally untidy."

16

The bow of the police launch, which for the past twenty minutes had been slanted at an angle of about forty-five degrees above the water, suddenly began to drop as the skipper reduced power. To our right, a junk with a single brown sail flapping in the stern altered course away from us. Ahead of us, still in the middle distance, I could just make out several police cars drawn up in a cluster beside the pier. They looked like tiny Dinky Toys against the massive backdrop of the Hong Kong skyscrapers. It was hard to believe that I had been away for no more than a few hours. Sergeant Li Sing climbed down a ladder from the small bridge and made his way back to where I was sitting in the stern.

"I've been talking to headquarters on the radiophone," he said. "There's quite a reception party waiting for you, ma'am. Half the police department seems to have turned out to greet you, not to mention the people from Government House."

"What about O'Grady?" I asked.

"No sign of him. They're watching the airport and

docks, of course, but the general view seems to be that he's left the colony already, probably by sea on a small craft. Even if we were able to spot him, it's highly unlikely that we would be able to catch him. Our pursuit boats have twin two-hundred-horsepower engines with top speeds of fifty-five knots, whereas most of the gangster craft can now do sixty-five knots. The trouble is that the Royal Hong Kong Squadron has not been allowed to modernize its equipment. It's all part of the rundown, I'm afraid. If O'Grady has gotten himself to Macao, there's nothing much we can do about it."

"If he has, it's certainly not your fault, Sergeant. You did a good job."

"Thank you," he said simply. "It's what I've been trained to do. I only wish there were more of my countrymen willing to try to make things work in the future."

Suddenly, an expression of doubt crossed his face. His bland Chinese features were contorted in momentary anxiety. "That's the way to look at it, isn't it?"

I searched my mind for some suitable reassurance to give him, but was relieved from having to do so by the sound of the ship's whistle announcing our arrival at the quayside. The helmsman was turning the boat in a wide circle to the left so that he could reverse into the dock. The reception party was now clearly identifiable. Standing erect beside Commander Bayliss was an army officer dressed in light khaki, with a stiff-peaked hat pulled firmly down over his forehead. The color of the band around the cap was the distinctive white of the Coldstream Guards.

I began to fumble in my shoulder bag for a mirror. By the time I had felt its rounded surface, the starboard side of the boat had bumped gently against the quay. It was too late to check my makeup. Simon Carey would have to take me as I was.

I moved automatically toward the exit point. As I scrambled over the side of the boat, Simon stretched down and pulled me firmly away from the rising swell.

"I'm glad you're okay," he said. "We've all been quite alarmed about what you've been up to."

"Thanks for being around when you were needed," I muttered. It was an unpremeditated gut reaction and as soon as I had said it, I regretted it. We had lost too much time together already. The last thing I wanted to do now was to waste whatever opportunities there remained of getting to know him better by quarreling.

As it happened, he took my reproach in good part. Laughing, he said, "Don't be like that. I've got a pretty good alibi, which I would be honored to reveal to you if you will have dinner with me tonight."

"Sounds great," I said, and squeezed the hand that was still holding mine. We parted sharply as Commander Bayliss came up to us.

"Welcome back, Lady Hildreth. Sergeant Li Sing tells me you've had an interesting afternoon."

"Very good policeman, your man Sergeant Li Sing," I replied.

"I'm delighted he was useful," Bayliss said. "He worked in my office for a year and was first-class at administration. I'm relieved to hear he's good on the beat, as well. Now, if you're agreeable, I think we should go back to my office for a proper debriefing. Are you able to join us, Simon?"

The guards officer beside me looked at his watch. "I think it would be a good idea if I did. I've got about an hour before the Governor wants to see me. That should just about give me enough time to get to and from your office, Malcolm. Why don't you come in my car, Jane? We'll all meet up in the commander's room."

As soon as we were seated together, Simon's driver began to move off in the direction of police headquarters.

We turned onto Harcourt Road; to our left, the harbor still bustled with late-afternoon shipping. The wind had dropped and a thin haze hung over the water. Suddenly, Simon turned to me. He looked tired. Dark rings circled his eyes.

"What a messy business this arms find is turning out to be." He sighed. "I'm not entirely surprised that your office has decided that your presence here gives them the opportunity to nose around a bit, but don't let it get out of hand. These really are very dangerous waters, perhaps more so than you realize even after today's events."

"Thank you for that fatherly advice, kind sir; but I am aware of some of the possible ramifications."

He chose to ignore the tartness in my reply.

"I did the homework you set me on your friends from the Cotswolds," he said. "What is the name of the village where they all live?"

"Little Bisset."

"Didn't you say you saw them all for the first time in the village church?"

"Yes."

"Little Bisset Church is Anglican, isn't it?"

"It certainly is—very orthodox."

He paused for a moment, then he said, "That's strange."

"Why?"

"Because both Mr. Wates, the schoolmaster-cum-former-soldier and Mr. Shawcross, the official who died a few years ago, were Catholics when they were here. As far as I can tell, so was Mrs. Shawcross, who you say is still living in Little Bisset."

I looked out of the window for a moment to where an old man sat cross-legged on the pavement. Beside him a few wristwatches were laid out in a neat row on top of a wooden box turned upside down to support them. How lucky I had been to have made contact with Simon before I had arrived in Hong Kong. He was a jewel. I turned away from the window to look at him. His face was more composed now. He must have known I was pleased with him.

"Would I be allowed to have a short chat with each of your sources before I leave?" I asked him quietly.

He frowned but his eyes were twinkling now. "What on earth for? Don't you trust me to have asked the right questions?"

I touched his arm. "Of course I trust you. You have no idea how much I trust you."

"But?"

"Man and woman are complementary to each other," I ventured.

"What on earth does that mean?"

"It means that a dual-sex interrogation team is the most formidable you can muster. Masculine logic matched with feminine cunning is quite unbeatable. You would get things out of informants that I never could, using hard argument. Vice versa, I would achieve things you wouldn't dream of."

"By oozing sex appeal at them."

"Strangely enough, it's got nothing to do with sex. If it's going to work, it does so on women just as effectively as it does on men. Our approach is to use almost the opposite of logic. We start with a hunch and lurch to the next hunch without the apparent need for any link between the two. Sometimes it works and sometimes it doesn't."

He raised his arms in mock surrender. "All right," he said. "I'll see what I can do. There's one chap at least who might be willing to talk to you."

We sat in silence for a moment, then I said, "Do you mind if I ask you a rather personal question?"

"I don't really know. Why not try me?"

"Do you have a girlfriend out here? A proper one, I mean?"

He looked straight at me and smiled. A curl of fair hair had fallen across his forehead.

"What's that got to do with murderous Triads?" he asked.

I must have looked cross and his smile burst into laughter.

"You know what, Jane, you sound just like my mother. She's always asking me about girlfriends, forever banging on about my settling down with someone nice. The trouble is, there's not much nice skirt on offer out here these days. If you ignore the tourists—and even they're a dying breed—you're left with Mrs. Longbotham in the office. At fifty-four, she's a bit out of my league."

"Your secretary?"

"Yes."

"I talked to her when you went AWOL. She didn't know where you were."

"Ah."

"Do I get to know?" I tried not to sound moody.

"What?"

"Where you were?"

"Later," he said. "Over dinner. You will come to dinner with me, won't you?"

"Yes, please," I said quickly.

At this moment, we came to a halt outside police headquarters. Commander Bayliss had arrived ahead of us and was waiting on the curbside.

"Welcome back officially," he said as he opened the door for me.

A few minutes later, we reached his office. "First things first," he said. "What I suspect we all need most at this stage is a drink."

I asked for tea. Simon and the commander ordered gin and tonics. The three of us then sat in a triangle around the coffee table.

"What the hell do we think is going on?" the policeman asked. "It's certainly a much grander show than we originally thought."

"It looks like a very big operation indeed," Simon conceded. "That's certainly the way that the Reds are viewing it."

Commander Bayliss looked at him with some astonishment. "Have you discussed this with the mainland Chinese already, Simon?"

"Of course, Malcolm, you know the drill as well as I do. They have to be the first to know about anything that is worrying HMG about the colony. Anyway, the place is now so riddled with their agents that these days they usually know what's going on before we do."

"That's why you had to leave town in such a hurry yesterday?" I asked.

Simon studied his highly polished black shoes and then said, "For some reason, our usual contacts weren't available on the island yesterday evening. So, on the Governor's orders, I went over the border."

"To Beijing?" the policeman asked.

"No, just to Canton."

Bayliss pressed him. "Did you go alone?"

"I took your Mr. Hui with me."

"Who?"

"The Wo Sing Wo minnow you caught on Lantau. The one the Governor ordered to be held by the army."

"Ah, yes." I wondered whether the fact that he had had to hand over this catch to the military still rankled with Bayliss. If it did, he disguised it well.

"Just as well I did take him along," Simon went on. "The Chinese got more out of him in five minutes than we would have done in five years. God only knows what they did to the poor blighter." He paused and sipped his drink. Then he continued, "Anyway, the bottom line is that it is quite clear that Triads have a game plan to spill a lot of blood on the streets of Hong Kong over the next few weeks and months. They are playing for much bigger stakes than raising their protection money. Believe it or not, they actually want to put themselves in some sort of a position to be able to barter with the Commies. The idea, apparently, is that in return for a few favors from the mainland Chinese, the Triads will help restore order to the colony as we run up to handover day."

"Cheeky bastards," Bayliss growled. "Think they can do my job, do they? Terrorize the population into submission in return for a few more dollars and saving their own necks. They must be pretty naïve if they think the Reds will honor a bargain like that."

"There's more to come." Simon spoke quietly and with authority. "All this is being done, as I know you have already suspected, Jane, with the help of our friends from Ireland. There is little doubt that the IRA bought the guns from the Libyans and arranged for them to be delivered here."

"The thing that has been puzzling me," I said, "is what the IRA gets in return. Money wouldn't be enough, however big a profit they were making. There would have to be a stronger reason than financial gain to explain why the IRA would deny themselves the use of weapons of the type and caliber of the ones you have found. Our information is that they consider themselves desperately short of weapons at the moment."

For the first time, Simon looked at me coldly, as one professional to another.

"What makes the IRA tick is not our problem," he said. "We've got enough on our plate just now preventing a catastrophic civil war breaking out on the streets of Hong Kong."

"Point very much taken," I replied. "We'll pursue that aspect of the matter back home."

"Thank you." The look of tenderness had returned to his eyes.

That night, we sat opposite each other in a restaurant on Peak Hill, high above Hong Kong Island. We ate oysters and chateaubriand and sorbet. We drank champagne and Mouton Rothschild and Latour. Throughout we were each deliciously in control of our emotions, or at least, we thought we were.

"I shall catch a flight home tomorrow," I said, "after I've met one or two of your helpful friends."

He sighed and said, "Probably just as well you're leaving." Then he laughed a little nervously. "We mustn't spoil this by doing anything silly tonight. I wonder if the day will ever come when we are both ready for a serious relationship."

"All I know," I said, "is that I want a really slow dance with you before we leave this place."

"I'd like that, too."

As if by our command, the lights on the dance floor suddenly dimmed and the hard-rock music gave way to a low, slow waltz.

"This is it," he said, and grabbed my hand. We began to move inexorably toward the music. As we reached the dance floor, somehow a space was cleared for us. We danced in a small circle, rhythmically and perfectly in time. He led and I relaxed. We pressed closer and closer to each other. We danced as if to the last post. Soon the Union Jack would come down for the final sunset. Closer and closer. I could feel every shape and contour of his body. We were both perspiring with excitement.

The next day, I rubbed his hand down my cheek and walked without tears through the glass doors of Changi airport.

17

Mike O'Flynn gave me a wink that under other circumstances might have been rather cheeky, but that in these was plain sinister.

"You've been very busy, Lady Hildreth," he commented, "very busy, in more senses than one."

"What does that mean?" I asked, and immediately regretted the question.

"It means that you very understandably managed to mix business with pleasure while you were in Hong Kong. You're a lady after my own heart. I would do the same myself if I wasn't rotting here as a prisoner of war."

I straightened the pleats of my skirt and looked directly back at him. He leaned back in his chair and inhaled the smoke from his cigarette. His return gaze was steady and unflinching.

"I assume you got paid for the arms shipment before we found it in Hong Kong," I stated.

His face remained totally expressionless. It was as if he had not heard what I had said. For a moment, we sat in silence. The effect was strangely relaxing. Neither of us seemed to be embarrassed by the peacefulness. I had consciously to remind myself that I was sitting in a top-security prison in the presence of potentially one of the most dangerous IRA operators in existence. Suddenly, he stubbed out his half-smoked cigarette, itself an act of some defiance in prison. He pulled himself up in his chair. When he spoke this time, his voice was low and menacing.

"You know what I've been thinking, Lady Hildreth?" he said. "I've been thinking that you're wasting your precious time here. I'm sure I don't know why you bother. Tell them to send you back to Hong Kong. You'd be much better off there, as I said before, in more senses than one."

It had now become a matter of some importance that this conversation should end on my terms. The time had come to take what we call in the business a "flier."

I said, "It might ease our conversation along if I was to tell you that we know that the Triads haven't paid you in cash; that, indeed, cash isn't what it's all about, not at least as seen from your point of view. As a matter of fact, we're now pretty close to understanding the precise nature of the trade. In that context, I just thought you ought to know, Mr. O'Flynn, that we're piling up enough evidence against you to keep you behind bars forever, and I mean forever."

I saw the fingers of his right hand tighten so that the whites of his knuckles shone across the table.

"Get off my back, lady, while you're still alive. I'm a little old-fashioned and I prefer not to fight dirty with women, but I will if I have to. You should know that. Think for a moment of what happened to your traveling companion, Anne."

Suddenly, he pushed back his chair and got up from the table that separated us. I braced myself. If he attacked me, I would have to defend myself. There was no time to call in the escort waiting in the passage outside. O'Flynn moved quickly and silently around the table. As he did so, he bent down into a crouch, low and wiry. Still seated, I coiled my back, tightening the springs of my muscles. Hatred oozed from his eyes as he closed the gap between us. I knew that he had absolutely nothing to lose by killing me.

Then, unexpectedly, as if responding to orders from some unseen command, he sidestepped me and moved toward the small barred window behind my back. He came a sudden halt in front of the window and for a moment stood staring down at the car park below. This time, the stillness in the room had a strange, unnatural quality to it. It was O'Flynn who again broke the silence. The pitch of his voice was so low as to be barely audible. "Let this be your last warning, lady."

At that moment, there was a deafening explosion outside the window. The whole room trembled with its impact. A light bulb crashed to the ground beside my feet. Beyond the bars and the thick panes of the window, a cloud of black smoke drifted slowly upward toward the sky.

O'Flynn turned slowly round to face me. He leaned back against the wall. His lips were stretched in a triumphant sneer.

"That was your Mercedes, that was, lady," he said quietly. "You'll either have to walk home to your pretty little cottage in Chipping Campden or else ask one of your policeman friends to give you a lift. You'll certainly never drive that car again, that's for sure. It all goes to show that you and I will each be better off if we remain friends. At the least, we would do well to keep a healthy respect between us. You stay on your patch and I'll stay on mine." His Southern Irish accent had become more pronounced in the last few minutes.

I stood up from the table and went over to join him beside the window. As I had suspected, he was slightly shorter than I. When I approached him, he turned and we both peered out between the bars. Below us, a prison officer was running over to the spot where my car had been parked and was now a pile of steaming metal, its frame blackened and grotesquely distorted by the force of the explosion. I sensed the man beside me move himself a little closer. Our contact had become almost intimate.

"The truth is that we can do what we like with you Brits when we choose." His voice was now little more than a whisper. I looked sideways at him. His eyes were shining with pride. A bead of sweat trickled from beneath a gray curl on the side of his head and rolled down his roughly shaven cheek.

I knew then that there was nothing uncontrolled or erratic about this act of IRA violence. On this occasion at least, they had known exactly what they were doing. I must be getting close to something very big indeed for them to risk the use of one of their precious mainland-based units to blow up my empty car. What's more, O'Flynn must have had some very strong reasons to have allowed himself to become the focus of attention. His whole career with the IRA had so far been spent studiously maintaining the lowest possible profile.

I adjusted the straps of my shoulder bag and said, "This conversation seems to have reached what one might call a natural break. I will call on you again if I need to, Mr. O'Flynn. In the meantime, if anything occurs to you that in your judgment might be useful to me and which you feel you would like to pass on to me, I'm sure you will bear in mind that my office is sometimes permitted to do a few deals."

My calmness seemed to annoy him. I certainly took his lack of response at least in part as a sign of his irritation.

As I emerged from the high-security interview room, a prison officer stood up from where he had been sitting on a bench on the opposite side of the passage. He began to move toward the door I had just come out of. I was about to give him a word of warning about O'Flynn's current mood, when the whole prison suddenly broke into a wild symphony of alarm bells and sirens. In a courtyard below, officers in white shirt-sleeve order were rushing from one side to the other. Dogs were barking. Orders were shouted. An Assistant Governor in civilian clothes ran past me toward a steep flight of stairs.

"A car has blown up outside the front gate," he called back to me.

When I reached the main entrance, I found it almost impossible to attract the attention of the controller. At last, after shouting my name several times into the intercom, the thick glass door began slowly to unlatch itself. Outside in the car park, smoke was still pouring from the remains of my car. As I began to walk toward it, two police cars with blue lights flashing screamed to a halt in front of the prison entrance. I noticed that one of them contained my friend John Andrews. An army lorry raced up from a road to the right. In the distance, I could hear the rattle of an approaching helicopter. Superintendent Andrews began to run toward me.

"What on earth are you doing here, Jane?" He panted as he caught up with me.

I pointed at the smouldering wreck. "As Mr. O'Flynn has just informed me—'That was my Mercedes, that was.'"

"Good God."

"Don't look so surprised, John. Mine is an exciting job. These things happen from time to time."

He looked hard at me. The twinkle was still in his eye,

although his round, open face was just a little redder than usual.

"I hope it was insured," he said. "You'd better get yourself a less conspicuous car next time."

I smiled. "I doubt if that would impress our IRA friends much, at least not the ones who blew this thing up. This was a heavily planned job. They had worked it out down to the smallest, most incidental detail, including the fact that I was not to be in it when the bang went off."

"Why?"

"Presumably because on this occasion they didn't want to kill me."

"What did they want, Jane?"

"All I can say is that if they wanted me alive, it is because they like what I am doing. Apparently they want me to go on with it with even greater enthusiasm than I'm managing at present. I suppose they must have made some sort of character assessment of me. By blowing up my car, they must think I'll press even harder than before.

"It is a bit tortuous, I must admit, but these boys don't bomb empty cars by mistake; and they certainly can't believe that by doing so they will frighten me off. I must have become some sort of useful decoy for them. It must suit them for me to be pursuing my present line of inquiries. All of which leads me to conclude that I had better get straight back to the drawing board and think again. I suspect it's about time to revisit Little Bisset."

Our conversation was interrupted by what sounded distinctly like a hunting horn. As it turned out, that was almost what it was. In all the excitement, I had totally failed to notice the arrival on the scene of the mauve 1930s Bentley. The horn was attached to the outside of the car on the driver's side. The driver was Patricia Huntington, dressed in green battle fatigue, which was pulled together round her middle by what looked like a Second World War webbing belt.

Pat steered the car in a semicircle around the car park and then headed for where John Andrews and I were standing. As she approached us, she seemed to accelerate. I thought for one awful moment that she had lost control of the brakes and that we were all to be crushed under her charge. The car was almost on top of the superintendent when it came to an abrupt halt.

Pat swung open the door and leapt to the ground. Her dark eyes were ablaze with the excitement of battle.

"My God, what a sight," she exclaimed, looking at my former car. I detected a note of relish in her voice. "I heard there was some fun about, but this takes the biscuit. Jane, you will need a chauffeur if they're going to make a habit of blowing up your cars. To start with, I thought you would probably need a lift home." Pat was nothing if not practical.

"I'm grateful," I said, "but how did you hear?"

"It was on the local news."

"That my car had been blown up?"

"No, that *a* car had exploded outside Top Marsden. I assumed it would be yours."

"You're wonderful," I said. "Let's go home now. I'm starving and there's so much to do." Turning to the superintendent, I said, "John, would you be a dear and deal with the paperwork and the prison authorities about all this. I have a feeling in my bones that it's going to be important for me to press on with the cause as fast as possible."

"It'll be a pleasure, ma'am."

He gave me a mock salute as I slid into the passenger seat beside Pat. As we lurched out of the car park, two more army vehicles drew up outside the prison. Several men in khaki uniforms jumped down from behind tarpaulin covers. Somewhere in back of the prison, I could hear the helicopter coming in to land.

Beside me, Pat Huntington's long white hair was streaming back, blown by the rush of wind through the open windows. What a beauty she must have been fifty years ago.

18

This time, as I sat at the back of the church in Little Bisset, I found the atmosphere sullen and oppressive. The vicar spoke in a tone that, in contrast to his style at the last service I had heard him take, was subdued and lifeless. Gone was the passion and the high theology. In its place was a rather suspicious and mechanical repetition of platitudes. The grand, and no doubt hopeless, crusade for the reconciliation of the churches had given place to a mealy-mouthed and cringing defense of the status quo. Even his physical appearance had changed. What had once been a fiery and fulsome red beard had shrunk into a rusty and untidy shrub of superfluous hair. There was a touch of the degenerate about him.

At the end of the service, I chose to leave ahead of the rest of the congregation. I stood for a moment in the graveyard, outside the Norman porch, waiting for the others to come out. The midsummer sun was reflected brilliantly in the evaporating dew and contrasted sharply with the gloom inside the church. Beyond the wicket gate, outside the boundaries of the churchyard, a young lad in his teens, who looked rather simple, sat cross-legged on a wall, staring vacantly into space. Standing by myself, with only this silent village boy for company, I was at peace with nature. It was almost a religious experience, and certainly more profound than anything that had taken place in church.

Possibly it was this inner contentment that made me so unprepared for my reception by the villagers when they began to drift out of church. Their attitude to me really was quite remarkable. As each one emerged from the blackened interior, he or she seemed to blink in my direction, then, making sure not to catch my eye, hurried past me down the path that led out onto the road. Not a word was said to me as each one passed me by. Mrs. Shawcross, forced into a slight stoop by her heavy frame; Christine Lewis, more thickly made up and thinly dressed than ever; bowlegged Mrs. Carver with her lanky husband; roly-poly Mr. Wates: They each scurried past me as if I were infectious.

The last to come out were Colonel and Mrs. Dalrymple. They followed behind a young couple with a baby, who were unknown to me. The colonel led his beautiful wife by the arm. They passed me in dressed file as if they were trooping the color. Each stared with a fixed look straight ahead. The effect was bizarre, to say the least.

Having watched them go past, I was just about to reenter the church to look for the vicar, on whom I had decided to force my attentions—unwilling though he might be to receive them—when something happened that quite definitely and dramatically broke the pattern of events.

Colonel and Mrs. Dalrymple had just reached the wicket gate at the end of the path. I noticed the colonel step back and begin to usher his wife in front of him through the gate and onto the road. Suddenly, and quite unexpectedly, she broke away from her husband and began to walk hurriedly back to where I was standing, still near the church door and under the branch of an old chestnut tree. I had no doubt that she was heading toward me, or that she wanted to speak to me. She looked straight at me as she tried to break into a run. She was only prevented from doing so by the high-heeled shoes she was wearing and by her tight black skirt, the lower half of a well-tailored suit.

Dalrymple, who had clearly been temporarily taken aback by his wife's unplanned-for action, quickly recovered and began to move to catch up to her. I decided it was time to react myself and hurried forward to join Mrs. Dalrymple. When we met halfway down the path, she was flustered and a little out of breath. Several strands of her lovely brown hair had fallen across her face. I saw for the first time that beneath her long eyelashes her eyes were full of sadness; so much so that for a moment I thought she might burst into tears.

She paused and looked questioningly at me, as if she had been suddenly struck by some fresh doubt about the wisdom of what she was doing. When finally she spoke, her words were well formed and clearly pronounced but the manner of their delivery was hesitant, even slightly bewildered.

"I say, I'm afraid I don't remember your name. I've never been very good at names. Philip always does all the introductions." She panted.

"Jane," I said quickly.

She looked at me blankly.

"My name's Jane." I tried to suppress the urgency in my voice. I could see her husband was approaching as fast from behind her.

"Oh yes. There is something you must know. I can't hold it back anymore."

She paused. The sorrowfulness in her eyes had given way to a sort of wildness. She didn't look very well.

"Yes?" I tried to press her, but it was too late. Colonel Dalrymple had reached us and had grabbed her arm.

"I'm sorry about all this," he said forcefully. "I'm afraid my wife is not at all well. I shouldn't have allowed her to attend church. Come on, old girl. It's time you were home."

There was a pleading look in his wife's face as he began to pull her back down the path. I was on the point of telling him that I would like to make arrangements for a formal interview with his wife when I became aware that someone was standing immediately behind me. I turned round to behold the unsmiling face of the vicar.

"Poor Mrs. Dalrymple," he said. "It's true what the colonel says. She's not well, not well at all. Indeed, she hasn't been really fit for some time. It's a great shame. She's such an attractive woman. Her illness is a great worry to the colonel."

"How long has she been like this?" I asked.

"Several months now. Very sad."

"She appeared all right to me the last time I saw her, which was only about two weeks ago," I said.

The vicar looked at me intently and shook his head. I noticed that his dog collar was dirty and that the long strands of his hair were greasy and unwashed. He seemed tired and uncared for.

"Still wanting to believe the worst of us. I'm sorry for that."

"I don't think anyone would have liked the way that Colonel Dalrymple dragged his wife away from me. She clearly wanted to speak to me and he should have let her. Now I shall have to go through all the formalities of an official interview with her, which could be much more of a strain for her if she really is unwell."

"I don't think any good will come of it," he muttered, and then, as an apparent afterthought, he added, "May I ask why you are back in our midst, Lady Hildreth? Your last visit very much unsettled my parishioners. They're not happy about your return."

"That much I was able to make out for myself," I said. "As a matter of fact, it was precisely about that that I wanted to speak to you, Vicar. What's bitten them? I can't say they were particularly friendly the last time I was here, but the treatment I had today was extraordinary."

He looked down at the ground and began to shuffle his feet.

"We're a very close little community here, Lady Hildreth, and we don't take too easily to strangers prying into our affairs."

"Come, come, Vicar. I would have thought that one of the remarkable features of this village is just how cosmopolitan its inhabitants are. Nothing parochial about this lot, at least not the ones I've met. Besides, it may have been forgotten by them, but a young Irish girl who was a frequent visitor here was murdered in the Cotswold hills only two weeks ago. I'm afraid it is inevitable, Mr. Sayers, that questions have to be asked."

"It's the questions you were asking about them last week in Hong Kong that has upset them most," the vicar said. He was staring directly at me now. His steely blue eyes were angry. I sensed I was in the presence of a very complex, and probably dangerous, individual. Nevertheless, I had no trouble meeting his gaze.

"Your parishioners are extremely well informed," I said, and turned to walk toward the 1940s Ford sedan that Pat had lent me until my Mercedes could be replaced. ("You'll have no trouble with this one," Pat had said, "I've replaced all its inards.")

· · ·

As I drove back to Chipping Campden, it was the enigmatic and mercurial character of the vicar that dominated my thoughts: his remarkable changes of appearance, his fiery and depressive moods, his theological theme of reconciliation, his ill temper, and the apparent loyalty to him of his parishioners. There was no neat package into which all this could be fitted.

When I arrived home, Pat Huntington was in a state of some excitement.

"We've had a busy morning here for once," she said. "In fact, this place has been like Hyde Park Corner. There have been so many vehicles driving backward and forward outside your house, that I thought at one moment of asking them to form a convoy. All the cars have been unmarked, but I have a feeling that most of them have been from the police. Your friend John Andrews seems to be in one of his protective moods. The other thing is that Frank has just come to say that there have been one or two rum characters asking questions about you round the pubs."

"Who's Frank?"

"He's a nice boy who's lived in the village most of his life. He's just landed himself a new job at the garage down the road. He's always been very helpful to me when I need spare parts."

"Ah, I see." People who found spare parts for Pat's cars were even more important to her than her old pals from the service who kept her in touch with all the London gossip. Being with Pat made me yearn for a moment to escape from a world that suddenly seemed to have become rather sinister and threatening.

"Did I ever tell you about Simon Carey?" I asked, kicking off my shoes and curling my legs up onto the sofa in my drawing room. "He was a teenage sweetheart who has grown up into something distinctly delicious. What's more, he never married." I closed my eyes. Through the haze of Hong Kong harbor, I could make out Simon standing tall and bare-chested against the flapping sail of an old junk. His golden hair was blowing behind him in the breeze.

"I'll go and put the kettle on." Pat's cheerful, matter-of-fact voice had the effect of bringing me back to reality.

"The only one I really can't make out is the vicar," I shouted to her in the kitchen.

"Old red beard," she called back.

"His beard was looking distinctly tatty this morning. I feel I may be getting the measure of the rest of them, but not him. He's too up and down, too changeable. I can't even make out whether he is the leader or being led."

"Leader of what?"

Pat had reappeared in the room carrying my Royal Worcester tea set, which she had laid out on a silver salver, a present from my late husband. John Hildreth had continued to remember my birthday even after we had been divorced. He had always been generous, at least about material and financial things. The magnitude of his divorce settlement is why I am able to live at the high standards to which I must confess I have now become totally accustomed. Looking back on him, the only problem with John was that, being one of the richest men in the world, he was quite simply spoiled.

"The direct answer to your question," I said to Pat, "is leader of the gang that killed Anne and that probably had a hand in the murder of poor Mr. Ho. I can't quite figure out yet how significant the vicar is. I am not even sure that he is fully tied up in it. His role is still one of the pieces of the jigsaw puzzle that is missing."

My open telephone rang on a small Chippendale table

beside me. Pat put down the tea set with a crash. I picked up the receiver.

"Jane?" a familiar voice asked.

"Speaking."

"John Andrews here."

"Hello, John. What can I do for you? Pat tells me that the protection you've been giving my house today has been overwhelming. Don't overdo it, for heaven's sake, or you'll have the Police Watch Committee on your back for wasting public money. I'm not *that* important, you know."

He ignored this completely. "Remember that Mrs. Dalrymple?" he demanded. "Her husband's a retired military man. They live in Little Bisset."

"Of course. As a matter of fact, I saw them both this morning. She was acting a bit strange."

"No more she ain't. I've just seen her corpse. Its head has been almost completely severed at the throat. And I said we were having a quiet summer."

I turned myself round on the sofa and placed my feet on the floor. "What do you want from me, John?" I asked.

"The husband, the colonel, has gone a bit potty. Can't say I blame him, mind. They say they were very close. Anyway, he's locked himself into his house, you know, the big manor building next to the church. The point is that he shouted at one of my constables about five minutes ago that unless you would agree to come and see him at once, he would blow his brains out with his own shotgun. So the question is, can you get over there pronto?"

"Of course," I answered.

19

I pushed the bell beside the white Georgian front door. There was no response. I wondered whether perhaps the police cars lined up in the road outside had frightened him. I pressed again and waited. This time, footsteps approached on the other side of the door. There were two low thuds as bolts were withdrawn. The door opened slowly.

Colonel Dalrymple was barely recognizable. His normally flat hair was wildly disheveled and seemed to have turned grey during the course of a few hours, but that may have been a trick of the light. The collar of his blue denim shirt was stained with what appeared to be blood. Some of it seemed to have spilled onto his fawn trousers. He wore slippers and his right eye was twitching. I cannot remember ever having witnessed such a transformation in a man in so short a time. It had, after all, only been that morning that I had seen him last.

His eyes were red and wet with tears.

"She was a good woman," he croaked.

"I'm sure she was," I replied gently.

He stared at me vacantly. For a moment, I wondered whether he had taken in exactly who I was. Then, as if reading my thoughts, he said, "You've been through my military files, I'm sure. There's not much about my wife in them. There should be. By God, there should be. I would have gone off the rails several times if it had not been for her. She saved me from myself. Things only started to go wrong when her health began to fail. You saw her this morning. She wasn't well."

"Who murdered her?" I asked.

The question had an immediate effect on him. He closed his eyes and began to cower away from me like a wounded animal. A trickle of saliva began to run down from the left corner of his mouth. The question seemed to hang over him like a knife. He appeared to sense that it would not go away, that I was ready to wait for a long time for a response. He began to retreat into a dark corner of the front hall, where details of his face became hard to make out.

Suddenly, he called out, "That's your business, you know it is." His voice was rasping and bitter.

"The same person who killed Anne?" I persisted.

"I don't know what you're talking about."

"Perhaps it was you, Colonel Dalrymple?" My eyes were growing accustomed to the gloom and I could see more clearly now how he was positioned. He was standing behind a heavy oak chair, his hands held flat against the back of the seat.

"Come here," he said. A note of cunning had entered his voice. "I want to show you something." I felt for the gun strapped underneath my jacket. He saw the movement of my hand and lifted up the back of the chair. I pulled out my gun and aimed it firmly at him.

"Don't try anything, silly, Colonel," I ordered.

At this, his manner suddenly changed again. His voice

became deeper and calmer. He appeared at last to have regained some sort of control over himself.

"I wasn't going to hurt you," he said. "You alarmed me, moving for your gun like that. I've been trained to react to that sort of thing. It was a reflex action. I'm sorry. You can put your gun away now. You won't need it."

"Very well," I agreed. "But you should understand that I am very highly qualified in unarmed combat. If you try anything at all, I shall not hesitate to use it. As I am sure you are aware, it can be quite painful."

I thought I heard him sigh. "Why don't we go and sit somewhere more comfortable," he suggested. "We don't have to stand in the hall like this. Let's go into the drawing room."

Some of his former courtesy returned as he led me next door and pulled out a chair for me. I returned my gun to its place under the left flap of my denim jacket and sat in the seat he offered. For a moment, he stood above me. Then he collapsed onto the sofa to my right.

"If you remember," I said, "this all started by your asking to see me. Apparently you have something to tell me."

"Yes." He seemed lost, as though he had forgotten what it was that had prompted him to summon me. He began to fumble in his pockets.

"I need a cigarette," he said. "I don't know where mine are. Do you have one, by any chance?"

I shook my head. "I gave up smoking some years ago."

"Will you come with me while I look for mine? They must be somewhere around the house."

"Of course." There was no question anyway of my letting him out of my sight until we had talked further.

We found an open packet of cigarette on the kitchen table at the back of the house. The kitchen itself was spotless and gave the appearance of not having been used for days.

When we returned to the drawing room, he said, "My wife trusted you."

"Then why did you stop her talking to me this morning?" I asked.

He drew on his cigarettes and seemed to relax a little. "So you think I killed my wife?" he asked almost carelessly.

"I didn't say that. I asked you whether you knew who did."

He ran a hand through his hair to smooth the strands back into place. With this gesture, he seemed finally to return to a state of some sort of normality.

"I didn't kill my wife, but I have an idea who did. The trouble is that I have no proof and I'm not the sort of man to make serious allegations without evidence. If I get it, I'll make sure you're one of the first to know."

"So what did you want to tell me?" My growing exasperation must have begun to show through.

"I'll come to that in my own time. It's what my wife wanted to tell you this morning. If I hadn't stopped her, she would probably be alive now. There wouldn't have been any point in killing her other than for revenge. You would have known all you needed to know. I suppose they expected me to keep it all to myself when she was gone. I don't think they thought I would break down. But they were wrong, weren't they? God, how wrong they were. You see, they never knew how much I loved her."

He turned and began to stare toward the door, almost as if he was waiting for an attack. Tears began to roll down his cheeks. I looked away from him. I do not like to see men cry, not, that is, unless I am in love with them.

There was a ring at the door. Perhaps he had been expecting someone, after all. From my point of view, it was a very unwanted interruption. I cursed silently as I saw him recoil nervously on the sofa. I thought of not answering the bell, at least not until he had told me what had been on his wife's mind outside the church that morning. The bell rang again, this time more shrilly, somehow with greater urgency.

I got up reluctantly and said, "I think we should go together to see who it is."

"I won't speak to anyone," he said.

"Don't worry, I'll do the talking." This appeared to reassure him. The man on the front doorstep turned out to be one of the young policemen whom John Andrews had sent with me. Having not heard from me for several minutes, he had become understandably anxious for my safety. I assured him that everything was fine and asked him not to interrupt us again. The lad blushed as I closed the door on him.

When he had seen who it was, Colonel Dalrymple had retreated on his own back into the drawing room. I was anxious to rejoin him as quickly as possible before the momentum of our previous conversation was lost. When I did so, my worst fears seemed to be confirmed. He was huddled up in a large Georgian chair, staring out of the window, apparently oblivious to my return. I noticed he was shivering.

"You were about to tell me what was on your wife's mind," I prompted.

For a moment, there was no answer. I began to despair that there would ever be one. We had reached a verbal cul-de-sac. I toyed with the idea of arresting him and taking him into the police station for formal questioning. It was possible that the shock of this action for a man with his background would have the required effect.

"Colonel Dalrymple, I must have an answer. At the

very least, you will have to tell me why you called me here."

Slowly, he turned toward me. His face was blank. His eyes seemed to have become disconnected from their surroundings. When he began to speak, it was with a stammer.

"The enormity of it, the enormity of it." He shook his head as if in disbelief of what he was about to say. "It was to be a terrible crime, terrible." His voice had gone very quiet.

"Colonel, I'm finding it a little difficult to hear you."

He was looking straight through me. It was as if I wasn't there.

"They planned to blow up thousands of people."

"Who?"

"The IRA."

"Where?"

He looked at me in surprise, as if I should have known the answer to my own question. Then he said almost casually, "London."

"Is this what your wife wanted to tell me?"

He nodded.

"Can we start a little further back, Colonel? Assume that I have no idea what you're talking about."

"The opening night of the Royal Tournament," he stammered. "In two weeks' time."

"The IRA plans to blow up the Royal Tournament?"

"It's too big a job for them to do on their own." He seemed to be warming to his subject at last. "They don't have the resources on the mainland. So they've got one of the London-based Triads to help them."

"I see," I said. "In return for the arms shipments to Hong Kong?"

He was silent.

I tried to calculate how many people would be likely to

attend the opening night of the Royal Tournament in Earls Court in the center of London: perhaps twelve or thirteen thousand. As it was Britain's top-ranking military show, key members of the royal family would certainly be there, as would senior cabinet ministers, not to mention many of the highest-ranking officers in the armed services.

As to why the IRA might be unwilling or, more likely, unable to do the job on their own, my department certainly believed that the Provisionals were currently numerically weak on the ground in mainland Britain. From their point of view, there were all sorts of good reasons to link up with the London Triads.

"I'm afraid there are now so many more questions I shall need to ask you, Colonel Dalrymple. Until we have discussed the matter much more, I must assume that you and your wife were directly involved in some way in this business. I must, therefore, ask you to come with me to the nearest police station where the facilities exist for properly recording our conversation."

He seemed almost relieved by this turn of events. It was as if somewhere inside him a boil had been lanced. A great responsibility seemed to have been lifted from him. He sat upright in his chair. Some of his former sprightliness seemed to have returned.

"Does that mean I'm under arrest?" The question was put crisply, as if part of a military appraisal.

"Not yet," I said. "That may come later."

20

"What I want to know," I said to O'Flynn, "is why you haven't tried to kill me yet."

"Not necessary, dear lady. You're no threat to us."

I have to confess I rather savored this moment. I knew I was about to shock him, to wipe away the boyish grin that no doubt on many occasions over the years he had used to win over the hearts of men and, perhaps more especially, women to his cause. The murdered girl, Anne, had presumably been one such person who had been seduced by those impish, smiling eyes. The moment had come to puncture his self-confidence, to expose him, and his organization for what they were, rotten and utterly amoral.

"I wonder if your opinion of me would change if I was to mention the two words *Royal* and *Tournament?*" I asked.

I could not have hoped for a more satisfactory reaction. The smile, as I had suspected it would, vanished. The soft glow in his eyes was replaced immediately by a glare of fanatical hatred. He rose to his feet and banged his fist on the table. For the first time since I had known him, he was showing open emotion.

"If I had had my way, you would have been killed as soon as you came into the picture," he shouted. "I could see you were just the type of bloody busybody who would get there in the end. The others, the stupid bastards, took a different view of you. They thought you were more use helping to lay false trails all the way to Hong Kong. They seemed to be proved right when you found yourself a lover boy out there."

There was a hard knock at the door. I saw a movement at the eyehole.

"I'm all right, thank you, officer," I called out, and turned to face O'Flynn again.

"Now that it's all out, I suppose I'm hardly worth bothering about," I said. "It's all too late, Mr. O'Flynn, isn't it?"

A smile returned to his face. This time, it was overtly false and rather sinister.

"You're lucky, Lady Hildreth," he said. "Lucky on many counts, not least because I don't believe in revenge for its own sake. It's a waste of time. Taking it out on informers and our own people who go bad is one thing: That's part of discipline. But what good will it do our cause if I have your throat cut tomorrow, which by the way could be carried out without difficulty."

I suspected he might be right on the last point.

"We should have done it two weeks ago. Now, as you rightly say, it's too late. We'll have to abort this operation. But never fear, we'll be back. We always are and always will be, until we have brought the British imperialists to their knees in Ireland." He was lapsing into rhetorical overdrive and this did not suit me at all.

"I didn't come for a lecture in politics," I said. "That's not my business, as you well know."

"Then clear off," he said. "I've finished with you." He sat down again, as if to confirm that in his view the conversation was at an end. I had to admire the way in which, even in these circumstances, he carried an aura of authority.

"It's not quite as easy as that," I replied. "We still have at least a couple of murders to clear up."

"I thought that was for the ordinary police," he growled.

"For obvious reasons, my department has an interest in satisfying itself that it knows all there is to know about how the killings actually took place." This sounded rather more prim than I meant it to.

"Why are you telling me all this?"

"Because I need your help."

"You must be joking."

"Hardly. Because if you won't help us, we plan to put most of the blame on you."

His eyes narrowed. "What exactly does that mean?" There was a new menace in his voice.

"It means that in the absence of any other information, we shall want to bring you to court at least on charges of conspiracy to murder a girl called Anne and a woman called Mrs. Sheila Dalrymple. There is also some question as to whether you ordered Anne to murder an as-yet-unknown Chinese person."

"I can see you're no lawyer, that's for sure," he said.

I raised my right eyebrow and said nothing.

"Perhaps I can help you, lady. It's like this. I've been stuck here for the past ten years in a British imperialist prison. They don't let you out from a place like this to organize for people to be murdered. What's more, they vet your letters, listen in to your conversation with visitors, spy on your chats with other inmates. Despite the workings of your fertile imagination, which I must confess for a bit of fun I have tried to play on during one or two of our chats in recent days, they make it quite impossible for the likes of me to run any kind of an operation on the other side of the wall. Any jury would understand that, even if you don't. I've led you along to believe I still have some sort of control because I've frankly enjoyed having you back here. We don't get many chances in this place to have cozy little private chats with a sexy piece of crumpet like you. Of course, it's suited me for you to believe I was still some sort of Mr. Big. The more you thought this, the more you would be likely to come back. Besides, I rather flattered myself that the bigger the villain you imagined me to be, the more you fancied me. Most women are a bit that way."

"Like Anne?"

"Now that we're talking honestly, and not playacting, I have to tell you I have no idea at all who this Anne is that you keep going on about."

"Okay," I said. "Let's go on playing games. I agree with you that it's much more fun."

"Turns you on, doesn't it?" he said, leering.

I ignored this and chose my next words very cautiously. I wanted to be as careful as I could be not to get an innocent man—if that was what he turned out to be—unnecessarily into trouble with the IRA.

"We've been talking a bit to your vicar friend."

I thought I sensed a new alertness in his face.

"Which one?" he asked. "I've known hundreds."

"The Reverend Thomas Sayers, who lives in Little Bisset and visits you quite regularly, I'm told."

"So what's new with the vicar? Are you telling me he's been cutting people's throats, too?"

"Possibly," I conceded. "Did you know, Mr. O'Flynn, that he spent several years of the early part of his career working in South Armagh?"

O'Flynn whistled. "Well, isn't that just dandy. And do you know what, lady, I don't care a fig if he did. It's of no concern to me. All that I do know is that he's a Prod."

"That's probably true," I said cautiously. "What is certainly a fact is that he was an activist in the civil-rights movement in Northern Ireland in the 1960s."

"Civil rights have nothing to do with independence," he said fiercely. "You're barking up the wrong tree."

"Then we come to the others," I continued.

"The others?"

"The other members of the congregation in Little Bisset. They're very interesting."

"Are they? I think you must have gone barmy."

"For a start, each of the ones I have got to know has strong connections with Hong Kong."

"I agree. That is interesting." He seemed to relax.

"Secondly, they each used to be practicing Catholics. That's even more interesting for people who now spend every Sunday in the month in the Anglican church at Little Bisset."

"Okay," he said. "I'm finished with you. If you don't go, I'll call one of the screws. We have certain rights here, even under imperialist laws. One of them is that you don't have to talk to visitors you don't want to see. And I have decided I don't want to talk to you anymore, so hop it."

"As far as you're concerned, Hong Kong might as well never have existed," I said. "Your interests have focused entirely on the IRA unit in Little Bisset, with its regular services in the church and tea meetings at the parish hall. It was at these that the death of thousands of innocent people was being planned every week."

I carefully controlled my anger as I stood up to leave him. I tried not to think of the grotesque nature of the mass carnage that he and the others had planned with so much cold care and calculation. Its scale, were it to take place, would be totally without precedent. In the history of the world, there would be nothing in peacetime that would even come close to matching its enormity. My job was not to dwell on these matters but to use every professional skill I possessed to make sure that the outrage could not occur.

Pat Huntington, however, was in a vengeful mood when I returned home.

"The swine," she hissed. "When do we start to make arrests? You'll need my help for that at least. Don't leave it all to Special Branch. They'll only make a hash of it. Nothing personal, it's just that no one ever puts the poor dears properly in the picture on these occasions."

"I'm not quite ready to make arrests yet," I said. "I still haven't got all the evidence I need to pinpoint the actual killers. Nor am I absolutely certain as to which one of them is the local IRA commander. It would be helpful to sort out both points before we start to bring them in."

"Better not leave it too long," Pat advised, "or they might start to do the old disappearing trick."

"I agree. I plan to wrap the whole thing up as soon as I have finished this delicious plate of smoked salmon you have so sweetly put in front of me."

21

I parked the unmarked car that I had borrowed from a Special Branch contact (as it was less conspicuous than Pat's vintage Ford) in an overgrown cul-de-sac at the edge of the village. I locked it carefully and walked up a footpath that I had identified on a previous visit as meeting my needs. It had the advantage of running parallel to, but out of sight of, the main road. By this route, I was able to reach the vicarage unseen by any villager. I climbed through a beech hedge and approached the dilapidated Victorian house from the rear. As I had anticipated, the back door was locked with a simple Chubb device. This gave me no trouble at all. Once inside, I stood still and listened for any sign of life. All was quiet. I made my way silently to the vicar's study. Pushing the door open with my foot, I confirmed that the room was empty. I went in and sat myself down in a wicker chair. I waited for about half an hour. Then, as I had expected, I heard footsteps coming up the drive. I got up and braced myself behind the door of the room.

When he came in, I caught him completely by surprise.

I sprang at him from behind the door, placed my right hand over his mouth, and with my left arm locked his behind his back until I knew he would be in some pain. Then I released him and pushed him to the floor.

"That was just an appetizer," I said. "If required to do so, I can produce plenty more. As a matter of fact, I quite like the opportunity to practice."

"What on earth is going on?" he whispered with his face pressed against the floor and his back toward me.

"Time for some proper talking," I said. "We know almost everything there is to know about you. What I want to find out now is whether you killed the two women."

He began to scramble off the floor. As he did so, he fought to regain some sort of dignity.

"I don't know what you're talking about," he said. "But I shall certainly make sure that your behavior is reported to your superiors. It's absolutely disgraceful that you should be able to behave in this way. There are still some of us around who will try to stand up to the secret police, even though you may have cowed the majority of the population."

"I think it's time, Vicar, that you stopped preaching and started to speak something approaching the truth. We know that you are O'Flynn's go-between. The question is, how far were you prepared to go for him?"

He stood for a moment shakily on his feet. Then he slumped into a shabby easy chair. He wove the fingers of his hands together and placed them on top of his head. This gesture seemed in some strange way to give him confidence. When he spoke again, his voice was quiet but firm.

"What you people fail to understand is that I am a man of peace."

"The murders?" I asked. "Were they in the cause of peace?"

He appeared not to hear me.

"My life has been devoted to the unification of the churches. It is a noble cause, don't you think? No, perhaps not, you're probably not a Christian. It doesn't matter to you. Well, it does matter to me. It matters above everything else."

"I'm here to do my job," I said. "I have learned to keep my feelings about God to myself. My task is to find out precisely how you came to be associated with the Irish Republican Army. That's all. We can leave the theology till another time. It's a question of priorities."

"I understand," he said wearily. His large frame heaved in the chair. "It's a long-established practice of the vicar of Little Bisset that he visit Top Marsden prison. My two predecessors did it, probably more proficiently than I." For a moment, he seemed to be having some trouble breathing. I wondered whether the treatment I had given him had inflicted more damage than I had intended.

"The only difference between my approach and theirs was that I went out of my way to meet the Catholics in the prison as well as the Church of England people. That's how I came in contact with the IRA."

"It was one thing to be pally with them; it was rather a different matter working for them," I suggested bluntly.

"It all started by my doing innocent favors for them. At least, I thought they were innocent. Then came the pressure, call it blackmail if you like." He unclasped his hands and wiped the sweat from his forehead with the back of his arm.

The time had come for me to spring the trap on him. Before doing so, I paused for a moment to take another look at him. He was wearing a dark green corduroy jacket and unpressed gray flannel trousers. His cream shirt was tieless and unbuttoned at the neck. His bloodshot eyes stared up toward me. It was hard to tell whether he was more angry or frightened.

"Who was your contact on the outside?" I asked. He knew it was the essential question and made an attempt to deflect it.

"I'm sure you know already." Now his voice was more nervous.

"Perhaps, but I'd like to hear it from you."

"Most of the people you have met in the village were involved."

"It's exactly what they did, the precise parts that they played, that I need to know. Let's start with the Dalrymples."

At this, he suddenly seemed to come to life. A look of horror came across his face. He leaned forward in his chair and gripped its arms.

"Why are you asking me these questions?" he asked. "I thought you knew all this. Please tell me you did. If they think I've talked, they'll kill me."

"Like you helped to murder the others."

"No, you've got it wrong. Perhaps you don't know that much, after all. Oh my God, what have I done? What have you trapped me into?" He began to sob, the second man I had reduced to tears in two days. I ignored his blubbing and pursued the questioning.

"I want to clear up one point about Colonel Dalrymple," I said. "Is it likely that he spied for the IRA throughout the 1980s?"

For a moment, it seemed that he wasn't going to reply. Several tears were chasing each other down his right cheek. Then quietly he said, "I have no certain knowledge. But it is possible, I suppose."

If this piece of information was confirmed, it would go a long way to explain the accuracy of the IRA's knowledge of our troop movements throughout the previous decade.

"What are you going to do with me now?" he whimpered.

"That depends."

"On what?"

"On how helpful you are. If I think you're going to be of real use to us, I shall arrest you, which frankly now sounds like your best hope of staying alive. If you have nothing further to offer, I may decide that there's not enough yet for us to pull you in. In this case, I shall have to reinterview the villagers, no doubt using some of the information you've given me already. Then I'm afraid I wouldn't be too coy about revealing my source if I needed to."

His shoulders gave a sudden twitch.

"I think I can be very helpful to you," he said, "but please take me away somewhere safer first."

"What I will need to know is who actually killed the two women. Are you in a position to help me with that very particular piece of information?"

He nodded.

"In that case, we can do business," I said. "But I should make it clear I am no longer in the market for generalizations. I want names, dates, events. I hope we understand each other."

The vicar stood up. "Will you excuse me for a moment while I put on a dog collar. I want to be taken in as a man of the Church." His public image still seemed to matter to him.

"Of course, so long as you won't be embarrassed if I remain in the room."

The prospect of being accompanied by a woman while he changed must have been a little strange to him, to say the least, but I gave him no choice. I wasn't going to risk his escaping from me at this stage.

22

Simon Carey flicked the ash from his cigarette into a green ashtray.

"What made you decide the vicar was telling the truth?" he asked.

"For one thing, he was too scared to do anything else. For another, everything he said squared up with what we already knew."

Simon took a sip of the whiskey and soda I had poured out for him and lay back in the easy chair. He gazed for a moment at the view from my office window. His soft, kindly eyes lingered on the rooftops, shiny from the overnight rain, then they focused themselves across to Buckingham Palace and finally came to rest on Big Ben and the Houses of Parliament.

Suddenly, he said, "My God, the security in this place is tight. I thought I was going to be arrested when I arrived just now. It's like something out of James Bond, it really is, Jane. Not even my FCO driver seemed to know exactly where we were going until he received instructions on the car phone. As for the speed with which we were ushered into your underground car park, I'm surprised the car is still in one piece."

I laughed. "Your driver may not have known where our office is, but you can be damned sure the Russians do. Perhaps that's why our opposite numbers in Germany advertise themselves in the telephone book."

"I'm sorry to interrupt you," he said. "Let's get back to business. It's what we're both being paid for."

"I agree," I replied. It was true that I had been given instructions to provide him with a full briefing of every aspect of the case that might be of use to the authorities in Hong Kong. I would be less than totally frank, however, if I did not admit that I found his presence a bit of a distraction. Somehow it was not quite the same thing as debriefing a fellow agent.

"As I say, the vicar has been helpful, but he's by no means the only source. Several days before we got him to talk, we had pinpointed one or two of the villagers as active Republicans. Getting the full picture on Christine Lewis was a particularly straightforward matter. This was mainly because O'Grady, her policeman friend from Hong Kong, was prepared to talk when we finally tracked him down to a bar in Hamburg. We did this, of course, with the help of the West German authorities. One surprise was that the relationship between Mrs. Lewis and Desmond O'Grady turned out to be a purely professional one. He was the IRA's main contact man in Hong Kong and she was his courier. It was as simple as that."

"Mr. Carver was her alternate. I don't think he was ever a true follower of the Republican cause. There is no reason why he should have been. He wasn't even Irish, although as we know, like the rest of them, he was Catholic. What made Mr. Carver tick was money. The only trouble was that he wasn't very good at making it. He was much better, in fact, at piling up debts. It must have been just about the time when these were beginning to catch up with him that he bumped into O'Grady. It looks as though he was given a few chores to do by the Irishman in return for cash. He may even have thought at the time that these were totally aboveboard. From then on, as far as we can tell, it became a straightforward matter of blackmail. In the end, Carver was in so deep that he couldn't get out, much as we think he may have wanted to."

"Let's see, who does that leave us with?" Simon asked. "Mrs. Shawcross, Wates, and the Dalrymples. That's about it, isn't it, leaving aside the good vicar?"

"Exactly. They also happen, by the way, to be the most interesting members of the gang."

I looked at his glass. "Would you like a refill?"

"Yes, please," he replied. "I'm parched. This place has that sort of effect on one. Spooks always give me a dry mouth."

"You seem to forget I'm one myself."

"You don't count as a spook to me." He laughed. "It hasn't escaped my notice, incidentally, that you're not joining in with the booze."

"Not while I'm on duty."

"What about after hours?"

"Is that an invitation?"

"Yes."

"Accepted."

I stood up and went over to the drinks cupboard. So there was going to be another opportunity to meet him off duty. It had all been settled so quickly. My legs were shaking a bit like those of a schoolgirl waiting for her first date.

I hoped I would manage to hide my excitement, as least for the next few minutes. I handed him his drink and sat down again. Despite my good intentions, the business at hand seemed suddenly to have become almost incidental. Perhaps, on reflection, it was just as well. My speech became rather mechanical and so helped to disguise any baser feelings I may have had. For a moment my sense of professionalism almost deserted me. I suspect my description of events became a little stilted.

"Let's deal with the schoolmaster next," I suggested.

"Mr. Wates?"

"Yes. On the surface, he's a bit of a nonentity. In actual fact, as we know, he was an army-trained marksman. We have recently discovered that he is also an explosives expert of some standing. With the wrong motivation, he is altogether a very dangerous man. His father and mother were both Irish citizens who came over to this country during the depression. We're not sure yet when they each died; nor have we found out exactly when Wates became a devotee of the Republican cause. We believe that the death of his parents and his joining the IRA were in some way connected. At any rate, by the mid-1960s, he had been planted as some sort of a sleeper in Hong Kong. We're not even totally sure how or where he picked up his IRA training. It may have been while he was serving with the regular Northern Ireland garrison in the early 1960s, well before the recent troubles began there. As you can see, we have had some difficulty with Mr. Wates. He hasn't talked much. Indeed, for much of the past week, he seems to have gone into a sort of silence strike. He won't even speak to his friends, whom we are currently holding in the same remand center."

I paused to look at Simon. He was staring at the floor, apparently taking in what I was saying, so I went on.

"Much about Mr. Wates still remains a mystery, but no doubt we'll unravel it in good time. What we have learned is that although he undoubtedly trained the killer, it was decided that he should not do the job himself. This was presumably because it was thought that he would arouse too much suspicion with the victims. The actual murders were therefore left to someone else. When you bear in mind that both Anne and Mrs. Dalrymple were the subject of a particularly vicious form of knife attack to the throat, and when I tell you who actually performed this act, you will appreciate that Mr. Wates must be a particularly proficient and imaginative instructor in the art of how to kill people."

Simon shifted in his seat. I could see that he was now becoming restless.

"Stop teasing, Jane. Who the hell did it?"

I drew my chair closer to him.

"Patience," I said. "It really is better that I go through the thing logically, through a process of elimination."

"Let's take our friends the Dalrymples next. They really were a very mixed-up couple. For a start, they were both English through and through. He is that most dangerous of human beings, the thinking soldier. We always watch out for those types in my business: the sergeant in the Education Corps and the Greek scholar who has done a crash course at Sandhurst and is heading for the SAS. They can be wonderful, like my boss, or they can be a potential menace."

"Your boss is wonderful, is he?"

"Yes, he certainly is. Now may I continue?"

He winked at me and smiled.

"At some point early in his army service, Dalrymple came to the conclusion that the unification of Ireland was the only way to ensure its future stability. From then on, he was fair game for the IRA, who used him ruthlessly and very effectively over a considerable period. Many of its most daring operations in the late seventies and eighties were planned on information provided by Dalrymple."

"And what about his missus? Where did she fit in?" Simon asked.

"A good question, Major. His relationship with his wife was ultimately, as we now know, his undoing. Despite the fact that her beauty led to a certain amount of waywardness on her part in the early years of their marriage, they were in fact very close. Apparently he kept her fully in the picture from the start about his dealings with the IRA. We understand that, after showing some initial reservations, she dutifully went along with it all. One theory is that she wanted to make it up to her husband for her one or two lapses from the marriage vows. Anyway, it all went along without much incident until the Royal Tournament project emerged."

"Did you know, by the way," Simon interrupted, "that both the Prime Minister and the Queen were to be there this year?"

"Yes," I replied rather curtly. "Our department has thought of nothing much else for the last few weeks. The impact if they had succeeded is too horrific to contemplate."

He added, "In addition to senior ministers and members of the royal family, half the top brass of the military would have been wiped out, not to mention potentially thousands of innocent spectators."

"I know, it's unbelievable. We always thought the Brighton bombing was the worst we would ever get, but this would have been in a league of its own. So much so, in fact, that when Mrs. Dalrymple got to hear of it, she began to crack up. What's more, her anxieties began to play on her husband's nerves. Working for the cause of unity in Ireland was one thing. Blowing up thousands of people, including the monarch, at an army show in the middle of the capital was quite another. Every tenet of his military training and background cried out against it. The two of them worked each other up until something had to give. In the end, as we know, it was Mrs. Dalrymple who publicly tried to come out with it, and she was duly executed by the IRA for her pains."

"Assuming that she wasn't killed by her own husband, that leaves only the vicar and Mrs. Shawcross who could have done it," Simon said.

"Each would have had the confidence of the victims," I said.

"So which one was it?" he asked.

"Who would you put your money on?"

"From what you've told me, the vicar doesn't sound as if he would have the balls to do it. Although he ran around for O'Flynn, he just doesn't seem to have the killer quality somehow."

"If you were right," I said, "that would leave Mrs. Shawcross. Cuddly, overweight Mrs. Shawcross, usually full of good cheer, stiring her jam and feeding her animals. It seems pretty unlikely that she would on two occasions worm her way into the presence of two ladies with whom she was on friendly terms, and at the right moment draw out a knife and silently slit their throats. And yet that is precisely what she did. The fact is that she is the most fanatical of the whole gang. As it happens, she is not Irish, but her husband was. He introduced her to the Republican movement, which he served latterly under O'Grady's leadership in Hong Kong. But it was Mrs. Shawcross who became the true believer.

When her husband died, the IRA became her consuming passion. It was as if she was determined to avenge his death. Certainly she felt she had nothing to lose by her obsession."

The light in the room had faded.

"Let's get out of here," Simon said.

23

"What I can't quite get straight in my mind is why did they pick on poor little Hong Kong?" Simon asked. "Why did this unwholesome gang devote so much of its time to our fading colony on the other side of the world?"

He looked straight at me. His intelligent brown eyes glowed in the half-light of the nightclub. His looks were sufficiently striking for several of the women in the room to glance our way from time to time. The dark tan of his face contrasted with the light blue of his shirt. His hair had been recently cut and was lightly brushed toward the back of his head.

"To answer that," I replied, "you have to go back to the 1960s and 1970s. At that time, Hong Kong was a soft British military target. It was certainly important enough to the British for the IRA to lay down contingency plans for some sort of operation to embarrass us."

"The wonder is, I suppose," Simon chipped in, "that they left it so late to have a go."

"That may be so. But men such as O'Grady and Shawcross and even Carver were not simply out there for the cheap gin and tonics. Although they were not actually blowing the place up, they were making financial contacts in the underworld in both Hong Kong and Macao. In recent times, both places have become quite a useful source of funds for the Provos, the largest outside the United States, as a matter of fact. There can be no question that the Carvers and O'Gradys of this world have been more than paying their way."

"So when did they really begin to play around with the Triads?"

"Not seriously until after the signing of the Sino-British treaty in 1984. At that point, the Triads and the IRA suddenly had a common cause. For very different reasons, they each wanted to stir up unrest against the British. For the Irish, it was a wonderful way of kicking their old enemy when he was on his way down. For the mobsters, as we know, it was a way of trying to save their own skins and of winning a place for themselves in the new order."

"Your glass is empty," he said. "Let me fill it up."

When he had done so, the champagne bottle on the coffee table in front of us was almost empty. Annabel's had been his idea, and as far as I was concerned, it had been a good one. Its sophistication and its decadent frivolity suited my mood. It was good for once to be surrounded by well-dressed and expensive people.

"And that's how the ghastly Royal Tournament plot came about," he said.

"Got it in one."

"You never did find out anything more about the Chinese personage the Irish girl claimed to have murdered?" he asked.

"Not yet. O'Flynn won't discuss it, of course. We are beginning to piece together some sort of a picture of the Chinese man who visited Anne when she was staying with the vicar and we are trying to match this with some of the Chinese gangland killings that have taken place in the past few months. In my view, it's all pretty hopeless. We don't even know whether the girl was speaking the truth when she confessed to a murder."

Simon leaned back in his chair and slowly raised a tulip-shaped champagne glass to his lips.

"Well, that's that then," he said. "I've got all I need. I can go back to Hong Kong now."

I looked at him in utter astonishment. Then I burst out laughing.

"You bastard," I said. "You dirty swine."

He raised his left eyebrow.

"I thought we were going to be friends," I said.

He began to smile. "We are, I hope."

"You've got two weeks' leave?" I asked.

"Yes."

"So have I."

"Well?"

He was leaving it to me to make the next move. Suddenly, I felt girlishly nervous. I was beginning to like him too much to get this one wrong. Would he think me outrageously forward if I put the question that was now burning in my mind? We both fiddled with our glasses, which were now almost empty. I couldn't hold it back any longer. I had to ask him. If he said no, that would be the end of it. We would not be meant for each other. And yet, this man was beginning to mean more to me than anyone had for a very long time. I might be risking everything too soon. Men sometimes didn't like to be rushed. Would it perhaps be wise to play the relationship a little longer?

I moved closer to him. Then I heard myself ask, "Can we go away together somewhere nice?"

His reply was instant, spontaneous. "Yes, please. Where?"

"I'm serious." There must have been a new note of anxiety in my voice. His reaction had somehow seemed too fast. I wondered whether he had really meant it.

"So am I; deadly so," he said. His eyes were shining and I knew then that he wasn't teasing me.

"Have you heard of Breakers?" I asked. "Or perhaps you would prefer to see my apartment in New York?"

"Breakers?"

"It's a rather posh hotel in Palm Beach, overlooking the ocean."

"Sounds good."

"We can fly to Miami by Concorde; be there tomorrow afternoon."

He looked at his watch. "This afternoon, you mean."

"It's one of the greatest hotels in the world," I said.

"I believe you. But won't it be very hot at this time of year?"

My excitement was rising to a fever pitch. I could almost feel myself already lying in his arms on the hot sand washed over by the Atlantic surf.

I grabbed his hand. "Yes, so we'll have the place to ourselves. We can go to New York afterward if you like."

"Afterward, I must get back to Hong Kong. We've got some problems there, you may remember. This leave is only meant to last two weeks, you know. By the way, what about clothes?"

"We'll buy them over there. Stop looking for excuses."

"I'm not. I'm just being practical. Do you always make up your mind about things as fast as this?"

"When I find someone I like as much as you."

"That's very flattering."

"I think I'm beginning to fall in love with you," I said.

A large lady sitting at the bar in a low-cut red dress with several layers of diamonds hanging around her neck stared in our direction. Her bosoms heaved.

"Aren't they cute?" she said to a little man at her elbow.